SARAH PURDUE

LOVE FLYING HIGH

Complete and Unabridged

LINFORD
Leicester

First published in Great Britain in 2017

First Linford Edition
published 2018

A catalogue record for this book is available
from the British Library.

ISBN 978–1–4448–3876–3

Published by
F. A. Thorpe (Publishing)
Anstey, Leicestershire

Set by Words & Graphics Ltd.
Anstey, Leicestershire
Printed and bound in Great Britain by
T. J. International Ltd., Padstow, Cornwall

This book is printed on acid-free paper

1

The car drew up outside the window of Rachel's ground-floor flat. One glance at her watch told her that he was on time. The first positive sign in the mire that was blind dating at the mercy of your best friend. Not that she was complaining, she told herself, as she took once last look in the mirror. She couldn't moan about being single and then ignore offers to be introduced to new people.

Rachel had closed all the windows on the warm, breezy summer's day, and her front room was starting to feel a little too warm. She was wearing her favourite maxi dress, which was covered in tiny pale blue flowers, and her Roman-gladiator-style sandals. Her hair, long and warm brown, which she considered her best feature, was loose and stylishly ruffled, just gracing her

1

shoulders. It was, she reflected, her go-to first-date outfit.

The sound of a car horn brought her back to the here and now, and she took once last deep breath before stepping out of the sanctuary that was her tiny flat. The car was black and new. That pretty much summed up what Rachel knew about cars. She crossed the pavement and opened the door, peering in before taking the plunge and getting in. The man inside smiled at her, and perfectly matched the photo that Beth had emailed her so that she would know who she was looking for — no red roses at the train station these days.

'Hi, Rachel?' The man's voice was warm and friendly, and his smile seemed genuine.

Rachel slipped into the leather seat beside him and smoothed down her dress.

'You must be Chris,' Rachel said; knowing she was stating the obvious but not sure how else to get through this awkward and sometimes embarrassing phase of the date. The truth was, she had been on a few dates where it had been blatantly obvious from the start that she had nothing in common with her match, and therefore had little to talk about save the weather. 'Or do you prefer Christopher?' she added as an afterthought. A few of her friends insisted on calling her 'Rach' — something she could live without.

'Chris is fine. You look lovely,' he said before turning his attention to easing his car out of the tight parking space he had found.

Rachel wanted to ask where they were going. The message she had received from Chris had said it was to remain a surprise, but that it would be outdoors. Rachel had thought perhaps a picnic, or a nice country pub. Both of those options were high on her best first-date options. Rachel's flat was on the outskirts of South London and Chris navigated the roads like a true Londoner. Soon they were on the motorway heading south. Another good sign, Rachel thought.

'So, Beth says you work in retail.' It was a statement rather than a question, but a relatively safe place to start.

'I think Beth is overselling it,' Rachel said with a smile. 'I work in an independent hardware store.' She watched, saw the surprised reaction, and smiled.

'It was my first Saturday job when I came to London to study. I needed work to pay the bills. Uncle Jeff was still in business, and said he was happy to have me back full-time.'

'Ah, a family business,' Chris said knowingly.

Uncle Jeff was no actual relation, but was a good friend of her dad's, and so she had always called him her uncle. It didn't seem like a relevant point to share with Chris. He glanced at her for a moment, clearly expecting her to reciprocate the question.

'What do you do?' Rachel asked, even though Beth had already told her.

4

'I work in the City,' Chris said with an air of studied nonchalance.

'Really?' Rachel replied; again, she had been on enough dates to know the routine and etiquette.

'Yeah, it's pretty boring stuff. Financial markets and all that; but it paid off the student loans, if you know what I mean?'

Rachel did know, of course. It had taken her more than a few years to pay off her student debt and it was only now, four years later after no luxuries, that she was able to start her Masters. Rachel knew that she should be impressed. A job in the City was pretty impressive. It just wasn't something that she could get terribly excited about. It wasn't that she didn't appreciate money; she simply didn't really get the need to accrue lots of it. Earning enough to pay the bills and do some of the things that you wanted to do, perhaps, but a high-stress job that completely ruled your life was not on Rachel's wish list. Beth knew this, but had insisted that Chris was not like the others — whoever the 'others' were.

Now that Chris had been asked the question, he seemed to be happy to chat away about his working life and all the perks that came with it. Rachel, for her part, was happy to listen; after all, there wasn't much that was particularly interesting about hammers and nails. She gazed out the window as the view became more scenic and less like London. Rachel had a love/hate relationship with London, and was always happy to get away — but equally happy when she returned home.

They left the motorway and were quickly winding their way round country lanes. Rachel's spirits lifted a little at the idea of being out in the countryside, and kept her eyes peeled for the kind of rural pub that all Londoners seek out.

'Here we are,' Chris announced and Rachel say up straighter in her seat. Her mind had drifted elsewhere, and if she was quizzed later she doubted she would remember anything of what

Chris had told her about himself. Rachel looked out of the window as they drove up a short drive. They whizzed past a sign so quickly that she couldn't read it, but on the road ahead were three individuals dressed in what looked like all-in-one tracksuits. Rachel's heart and stomach sank. They reached a low, squat building, and when Rachel stepped out of the car she could see that beyond it lay a hangar and a runway.

She rested a hand on the door of the car to stop her jellied legs giving way beneath her. 'Beth,' she muttered with a grimace, 'I'm going to get you for this,' as her eyes looked at the sign above the low building: 'South Downs Skydiving Club'.

'We're going to do a tandem skydive!' Chris announced as if it was the best idea he had ever had.

2

There were a few issues with this first date, Rachel thought as she reluctantly followed Chris in through the door. Firstly — and this was probably the biggest one — Rachel was afraid of flying. And that didn't get near to how bad she was with heights. She sighed. She had known, almost as soon as she got in the car, that Chris was not going to be 'the one', but she had tried to remember Beth's advice: 'Don't give up too easily. Sometimes you need time to get to know someone before you decide.' And so, Rachel had given Chris the benefit of the doubt, but now she knew for sure. Chris expected her to jump out of a plane, and there was just no way *that* was ever going to happen. Past experience told her that when a first date was organised around an activity that you were going to refuse to do . . . well, let's just say it didn't bode well.

There was a small queue of people waiting to speak to a woman with wild hair who was standing behind the counter. Everyone in the queue, judging by the noise levels, was beyond excited at the idea of jumping out of a plane with only a bit of fabric to prevent them from crashing to earth. A piece of fabric, Rachel reminded herself, that you had to have the presence of mind to actually release at the right moment, assuming that the sheer terror didn't make you pass out. Rachel sniffed. Let them have their fun, she thought. It was good that some people enjoyed this kind of thing . . . but it didn't mean she had to feel bad that she would rather have a root canal at the dentist's.

'Now they need to know your weight and you have to sign an insurance waiver.' Chris said grinning at her, clearly not interpreting Rachel's facial expression as anything other than barely withheld excitement. Rachel grimaced.

'Now, I know women worry about men knowing how much they weigh,' Chris said, in a voice which suggested he was a guru when it came to women. 'So you can step on the scales, and I promise I won't look.'

Rachel stared; she couldn't help it. But only one word came to mind, and that was 'Really?'. She didn't even know where to start with that statement; but before she had a chance to say anything, the women with wild hair grabbed her arm and frogmarched her onto a set of scales.

'We don't rely on what people tell us anymore.' The woman grinned. 'They usually lie, and it's not good when how much you weigh factors into when you need to release the 'chute.'

Rachel kept her eyes fixed on the scales. It seemed the thing to do in the circumstances, and gave her something to focus her mind on as she fought the urge to pass out. The scales told her, in bright red numbers that she weighed nine stone, six pounds. Since Rachel never weighed herself, merely assessed whether her clothes still fitted, she was neither surprised, horrified nor delighted.

'Right then,' the woman said, making a note on a clipboard before handing it to Rachel. 'Take this and go through that room there. They will find you a flight suit that fits.' Rachel opened her mouth to say there was no need, but a shove to her back from the woman told her she needed to move out of the way.

Rachel stepped into the room which seemed to connect the low building to a corridor to the hangar and found herself with several other women. A man who looked bored was handing out flight suits. It seemed that you got what you were given. He looked Rachel up and down, and then handed her a black suit with bright pink flashes that looked like go-faster stripes. A shout from the front office and the man disappeared, at which point all the other women started to strip off. Rachel just stared — surely you didn't go skydiving naked under a suit that had been worn by goodness knew how many other people?

With colour rising in her cheeks, Rachel realised that the rest of the group were now staring at her, and so she tore her gaze away and looked at her suit. It couldn't hurt to put it on. She was sure that some people must chicken out after the safety briefing . . . surely there *was* some kind of briefing? Rachel noted that the other women had stripped down to leggings and t-shirts, and so she pulled off her dress, embarrassed that she was dressed so inappropriately, and knowing that she was going to be the only one skydiving in her bra and pants. Shaking her head, she firmly reminded herself that it didn't matter, since she wasn't *actually* going to go skydiving. No, Rachel was going to watch *Chris* jump out of a plane; and whilst she was waiting for that event to happen, she would have a coffee — assuming that there was somewhere round here to get one.

The other women had gone back to ignoring her, and were now swapping war stories about various high-adrenaline activities they had chosen to take part in. Rachel felt more like a fish out of water than ever but followed them, distracting herself with rehearsing what she would say when she gave Beth a piece of her mind. They walked along the corridor that linked to the main hangar and through a pair of swing doors. In the hangar, there were a number of small aircraft in various states of disrepair, and a long trestle table that seemed to hold the parachutes. Not knowing what else to do, and unable to find Chris, Rachel followed the group.

An older man, with rugged features that spoke of a life spent outdoors, stood in front of the table.

'Welcome to the South Downs Skydiving Club. Today most of you will be undertaking your first tandem jump. That means that you will be jumping with one of our experienced instructors.' The man threw his hand sideways, and the groups swivelled their eyes to take in a collection of suited individuals wearing helmets.

'Now, I know that some of you must be scared, but let me reassure you that there is nothing to worry about. All of our guys have clocked hundreds of jumps and are highly trained.'

Rachel held back a snort — as if any of that was going to convince her! Then the man began the safety briefing, which to Rachel's ears seemed to consist of a description of all the things that could go wrong, and ended with asking them each to carefully read the waiver before signing it. Rachel watched as everyone eagerly queued up to sign away any chance they would have of suing the organisation if something bad were to happen. She couldn't quite believe that all these people seemed happy to do that willingly. There was no way she was . . .

'Come on, Rach!' a voice said. Rachel knew it was Chris, and knew she should have told him that she hated it when people tried to shorten her name — a name which had not been created to have a shorter 'cute' version.

'It's Rachel,' she said under her breath.

'If you don't sign the form, you can't come,' Chris said, as if she were a donkey and he were dangling a particularly attractive carrot under her nose.

'It won't be much of a date if we don't both jump,' he added, looking a little concerned now at her lack of enthusiasm. Although the mean part of Rachel wondered if this was just because they had already been told there were no refunds.

'Rachel, is it?' The older man had walked over, distracted by the clipboard in his hand. 'This is Jack — he will be your tandem jumper today.'

Rachel froze and shook her head.

Nope, it couldn't be. I mean, she thought, if you did a survey of how many Jacks there were in the UK, there would be thousands — more likely, hundreds of thousands. What were the chances that this date could get even worse?

3

As it turned out, the chances of the date getting worse were extremely high. Rachel looked up — and then up some more — into her jumping partner's face. And it wasn't just any face. It was Jack's. At one time he had been *her* Jack, but that was before. Before it all went horribly wrong. The expression on Jack's face told her that the past had not been forgiven, and that his memories of her were as fresh as hers of him.

'Miss, you need to sign the waiver if you are going to jump. We can't wait for you forever.'

The words might, on the surface, have seemed benign, but the meaning was not lost on Rachel.

'I think Rachel here is having doubts,' Chris said. 'Can you use your legendary powers of persuasion on her, bud?'

17

Bud? Rachel thought. This really was one of those days that could only get worse. Not only was Jack here, but he and Chris seemed to know each other. How could Beth do this to her? Chris clapped her on the back and walked off, as if her signing the form was a formality that he could leave to his 'bud' Jack.

'I thought you were scared of heights,' Jack said coldly. Rachel looked up at him and properly took in the face that had been so familiar. It had been so long, but Jack hadn't changed. He wore his sandy-blonde unruly hair long, and his chiselled features were unshaven, with a two-day-old nearly-beard. He was tall, much taller than Rachel's five-foot-five, and lean. Rachel realised she had been asked a question.

'Or have you changed that much?' Jack added, his face crumpled by a frown.

Rachel wanted to open her mouth and shout at him. She hadn't changed, and he wasn't the only one who was still hurting. She hadn't been on a date in forever, but Beth had gathered together a group of her friends for what she called an 'intervention', and insisted that she stop wallowing and 'get out there'. Rachel had reluctantly agreed. It had seemed a bad decision then, but now — well, now it felt like the second worst decision she had made in her life, as she found herself staring up at the *single* worst decision she had ever made.

Jack was glaring at her, and Rachel could feel other eyes on her too. Chris, thankfully, seemed oblivious to the non-argument that was happening, as he was deep in conversation with his jump partner. But the rest of the group was giving them their full attention.

'Right, we ready, people?' the older man said as he walked back in from the office. 'Plane is fuelled and ready to go. Last chance to drop out,' he added with a grin; the group cheered, and it was clear that no one was chickening out.

'Well? Or are you too scared?'

Jack was provoking her, Rachel knew it. But to use those words, the words he had used the last time she had seen him . . . well, that was too much. She snatched the clipboard off him, scrawled her signature on the dotted line, and shoved it back at him so he had to take a step backwards before she realised she what she had done. For a split second, Jack seemed speechless and trapped. He looked down at the signature and then up at Rachel before wordlessly handing the clipboard to the woman with wild hair who had suddenly appeared at her shoulder.

'You alright, Jackie?' she said, almost purring.

Now Rachel felt like glaring. Jack was attacking her, but it seemed he had happily moved on, and she wondered if his anger and hurt were all an act. Rachel turned on her heel and stalked away from Jack, needing to put distance between him and the wild-haired woman. When she reached the group, they were just heading out through the open bay doors.

'Rach!' Chris shouted above the noise of the plane engines. 'I was getting a bit worried that you weren't going to do it.'

Rachel was aware that Jack had joined them and was surreptitiously studying their interaction, so she threw all her usual caution to the wind and wrapped her arm around Chris's waist. Chris didn't seem at all surprised at her sudden show of affection, and merely slipped an arm around her shoulders, pulling her in so that he could place a kiss on the top of her head. Rachel fought the urge to disentangle herself from his embrace — this was, after all, a first date; even if it was a date in which he had thought it was appropriate for them to throw themselves out of a plane — but she had started this, and couldn't really blame him for responding in kind. Not to mention the fact that she was sure Jack was still glowering at them.

Knowing that Jack was watching her

every move was enough to briefly distract Rachel from the stark reality that she had just signed up to not only get into an aeroplane — something she had sworn she would never do after that disastrous first and last time — but also to then jump out of it. And, as if things couldn't possibly get any worse, she was going to have to jump out of a plane attached to the man who she had once loved more than anything, but who had broken her heart. She risked a glance at Jack; unless he usually scowled his way through what he had always claimed was his favourite hobby, he wasn't so chuffed at the idea either.

Chris climbed into the small door first and then turned, chivalrously holding out a hand to help her in. The step up was too high for Rachel; she knew there was no way she could do this and keep her dignity, but she was going to try. She managed to hook one booted foot onto the edge of the doorway, and then all she could do was hope that Chris was strong enough to pull her aboard. Considering how the day was going, it should not have been a great shock that he wasn't. He pulled, and clearly seemed to think that she would somehow magically fly up into the plane, but instead she could feel herself teetering, one hand in Chris's and her foot about to lose its tenuous grip. She heard a sigh behind Chris's shoulder; before she could argue, Jack appeared beside him, and between them they hauled her inside and dumped her onto the floor.

There were no seats inside. Just ropes with small handles attached. The door was shoved closed from the outside, and Rachel listened as the handle was pulled into place. The engines revved and she lurched forward as the plane started to move. It wasn't going very fast, but Rachel could already feel the panic rise up inside her. The walls were pressing in on her and she felt like someone was squeezing the air from her chest. Her heart pounded in her ears and she wondered if the skydiving school provided the little airsickness paper bags that you got on ordinary flights. A quick glance around told her no, they didn't.

Rachel could only watch in wide-eyed, frozen fear as the instructors strapped on the backpacks which held their parachutes, checking straps and clips were fastened. The instructors then turned to their jumping buddies and clipped their harness to the fronts of their own.

Jack made his way over to her, and Rachel tried to swallow, but her mouth had gone suddenly dry and she was sure she had a whole bunch of black spots doing a tango in front of her eyes. His hand found hers and pulled her to her feet. Jack sat down and Rachel frowned — why was he sitting on the floor? Then she realised he was merely doing what everyone else was, and so even though she wanted to protest, she knew she couldn't as he pulled her onto his lap. She felt him attach the harness to the straps that criss-crossed her body, and was pulled back as he tugged on each one to check they were secure.

'You up for this?' Jack said, and even with the loud droning of the engines, Rachel could make out the challenge. 'Chris will understand if you decide not to,' he added, looking over his shoulder at Chris — who, not being able to hear the words, simply grinned and held up both thumbs. Rachel forced herself to smile weakly back.

'I said I was, didn't I?' she replied, finding that spark of anger that had lain dormant and using it to fire up her body, to make it respond to her. She was going to do this. She was going to show him.

4

She was going to do this and she was going to show him. The only problem with that sentiment was making her hands loosen their iron grip on each side of the door.

'If we're going to do this, we have to go now,' Jack's voice sounded above the scream of the wind. 'Or we miss the drop zone and risk . . . '

Rachel didn't want to hear any more about risk, so she abruptly let go; and before she could even process that her body had finally obeyed her, she was falling. She knew she was falling fast, but the tiny green fields below her seemed to be moving towards her at an alarming speed. Part of the safety briefing repeated in her head over and over: 'The brain can't process distances over two thousand feet, and so even if you are at twelve thousand, it will look just the same.' Weird, Rachel thought, that her brain was stuck on such a thing.

What she also realised was that she was holding her breath. The air felt like it was attacking her face and so she couldn't open her mouth to take any in. The panic that had momentarily disappeared as her brain tried to process the fact that yes, she really had just jumped out of a plane, and yes, she was now falling towards the earth, was now back in full force. There was nothing else for it; she had to close her eyes. Had to block out the fast-approaching ground. Of course, all her other senses told her she was still falling, but being unable to see her ultimate destination was oddly comforting.

For someone who hated aeroplanes, she had never wanted to be back inside one so badly. The air was not only attacking her face, but also her arms and legs, which felt like they were attached to the strings of her puppeteer and being pulled in random directions. Rachel felt hands on her arms, and for some strange reason she felt the panic tell her to fight them off, as if some great flying monster was attacking her. The hands squeezed and released; somehow Rachel's brain managed to process that of course they belonged to Jack, and that perhaps they were trying to help. She felt the pressure of the hands again, pulling her hands and arms out, which she dimly remembered from the briefing. Her legs seemed to get the message too, and they bent at the knee.

Rachel wasn't sure if it was her imagination, but it was like the puppeteer's strings had been cut, and she was once again in charge of her body. If you could ignore the 'hurtling through the air' bit. She felt Jack's chest rumble against her back and knew that he was laughing at her. Apparently her gut-wrenching fear was amusing to him. The fact that every cell in her body was screaming at her that she was about to die an extremely gruesome death was something he found funny. A small part of her mind that was apparently still rational told her she was being unfair. He had never revelled in anyone else's fear. In fact, at one time she would have said he was the only person in her life who truly understood her; but unfortunately the terrifying experience was squashing the rational voice to a high-pitched squeak that she could no longer hear, and all she was left with was the anger and resentment.

The anger made her open her eyes and the fear made her close them again. With no warning at all, Rachel wondered if her wish had come true. She felt like she was being dragged upwards. The sensation passed quickly, and she risked a swift glance upwards, beyond Jack's face — which displayed no fear, only exhilaration and sheer joy, Rachel could make out the plumes of the white and gold parachute as it caught the wind and started to slow their descent.

'Isn't this amazing?' Jack said. Or at least Rachel figured those were the words his mouth was trying to form, the sound being snatched away by the force of their fall. One glance at the earth hurtling towards her, and she felt a whimper escape her lips. She screwed her eyes up tight.

'Open your eyes,' Jack's voice demanded; Rachel managed a peek, but forced them shut again with a groan as the ground sped towards her.

'Lift up your legs.' Since his last suggestion had been such a poor one, Rachel decided to ignore him.

'I mean it, Jelly — legs, do it!' He was yelling now, and somehow had managed to lean in and aim directly into her ear. Her brain, however, was indignant that he was using the pet name he had for her. The pet name that she had secretly hated, but loved him enough to never tell him. The pet name he had no right to use right now. And then they hit the ground. Rachel flailed, making contact with the front of Jack's shins, and they collapsed in a heap of tangled limbs before the parachute floated down and smothered them.

For what felt like an age, Rachel just lay there. Her brain seemed frozen, like a computer screen when the mouse didn't work. It was if the experience she had just been through had completely overwhelmed her and everything had shut down. She felt unable to move her arms and legs, and it was then that the panic set in. Of course she couldn't move. People who jumped out of planes must frequently damage their backs. You could fracture your spine falling off a horse, for goodness' sake. And so in a fit of pique, to try and prove someone wrong, to get some form of twisted revenge, she had fundamentally changed her life forever. For starters, there was no way she could stay living where she was; there was no way she would be able to get a wheelchair through the front door . . .

'Rachel, for goodness' sake, move! You're killing me here.'

Rachel opened her mouth to reply, to tell him she couldn't move because she was seriously injured and it was all his fault. She felt a slight flash of shame since she knew deep down that last bit wasn't actually true, however true it felt in that moment. And then she realised that, unconsciously, her limbs were starting to move. They were following the last instruction, even though her brain had yet to catch up. She rolled to one side onto a tangle of ropes and parachute just as her brain started registering shouts from outside the cocoon they found themselves in. The shouts were soon followed by people outside pulling on the parachute fabric, and then suddenly the safety-talk guy appeared.

Rachel had now managed to sit up, and Safety Talk was by her side.

'You okay, Rachel?' he asked, running hands around her neck and down her back. 'Any pain anywhere?'

Rachel by now was registering that there was no obvious pain, and was testing out each of her limbs.

'I think I'm fine,' Rachel said, the sense of relief so intense that she could feel herself start to cry.

'Of course she's okay,' came another voice that, despite its exasperation, Rachel knew was Jack's. 'She wouldn't lift up her legs so I had to come in at an angle. I took the full force of the landing.'

The cocoon was suddenly lifted completely as others grabbed the edges of the parachute and pulled it away from them. The light that flooded her seemed so bright that Rachel threw up a hand to shield her eyes. She still felt too stunned to do very much, and could only watch as Safety Talk started to check Jack out for injuries. When he reached Jack's knee there was a yelp of pain, and that was enough to cut through the fog that had dampened Rachel's reactions. She managed to find her feet and was by Jack's side in an instant.

'Are you okay?' she said, filled with

both concern and more than a little guilt.

'Do I look okay?' Jack asked through gritted teeth, and it was then that Rachel could see how pale he was, and the beads of sweat that were gathering at his temples.

'You need to lie still, mate. I'm not sure about this knee, and we'll get a neck brace just to be on the safe side. The ambulance is on its way.'

Rachel stayed crouched by Jack's head whilst they carefully placed a rigid plastic brace around his neck and covered him in blankets. Despite the warm day, Jack was shivering. Rachel wanted to reach out and hold his hand, to offer him some comfort, but the fear that he would angrily reject her was too strong, and so instead she simply stayed where she was and tried not to wring her hands too much. Someone threw a blanket around her shoulders — it was Chris, but she couldn't take her attention off Jack long enough to acknowledge his act of kindness. For

Chris's part, he seemed unbothered, and instead knelt at Jack's side, grabbing his hand and giving it a squeeze.

'You'll be alright, mate. It's probably just a sprain.'

But Rachel could see the concern on Chris's face too, and it did nothing to quell the all-too-familiar sense of guilt.

5

Rachel kept looking out towards the road, and was the first to spot the ambulance.

'I see them,' she said out loud to no one in particular, before pointing out the blue flashing lights. Safety Talk looked up.

'Do you feel up to running down and directing them, love?' he asked.

Rachel nodded and forced herself to stand up. Her legs protested that they weren't ready to stand, let alone run, but her determination ordered them to do her bidding. With a wobbly start and a flash of concern that she was going to fall over, she put one foot in front of the other, and soon she was running to what she now realised was the edge of a field. She clambered over the stile and started to run, and then skidded to a halt. The field was full of cows who looked up from their munching of grass to stare at her. The cow nearest to her seemed particularly interested and slowly wandered in her direction. Rachel looked over her shoulder to the stile and the safety of the field beyond, and then back to the cows, which now seemed to be forming a sort of queue to come and inspect this interloper and the blue flashing lights beyond.

'You can do this,' Rachel told herself, saying the words out loud. It wasn't as if there was anyone else around to hear her, unless you counted farmyard animals. 'Jack needs you to do this.' And so, with gritted teeth and clenched fists, Rachel took a step and then another.

'Nice cows,' she said, wondering if they could understand. 'I would love to stay and chat.' She directed this comment to the lead cow. 'But I have a friend who really needs the help of those nice ambulance people over there'. The lead cow blinked, and

Rachel took that as understanding as she gingerly wove her way between the congregation of cattle.

'You alright, love?' called a tall and gangly man, dressed in the green outfit that paramedics wore.

Rachel nodded.

'Parachute accident?' the other asked, a woman who managed to look beautiful despite the green fatigues-like uniform.

'Have you got any pain anywhere?' continued the male paramedic, whose badge said 'Greg' on it.

Rachel shook her head. 'It's not me. We need to go back over there.' She pointed across the field of cows and swallowed. 'My instructor has hurt his knee. It was a bad landing,' she added by way of explanation. 'They think his neck's okay, but they've braced it just to be sure.'

Then all Rachel could do was watch as they gathered up a variety of kit.

'Lead on,' the woman said, carrying a metal stretcher under one arm and a large orange fluorescent bag under the other.

Rachel looked back at the cows, who had returned to their grazing, and started to make her way through the cattle-infested field, thinking all the while that at least if something happened she would have medically trained personnel to help her straight away. They reached the stile without incident, but followed by many curious bovine eyes, and were soon back with Jack. The paramedics launched into perfectly coordinated action and it was, Rachel reflected, quite a thing to watch. She felt some of the panic and guilt ease as she knew that Jack was being taken care of.

'I want to follow the ambulance to the hospital so I can take Jack home. Are you okay to ride in the ambulance with him?'

Rachel tried to hide the little jump she made at the sound of Chris's voice. She had been so wrapped up in watching the assessment of Jack, not to mention wincing whenever he did, that she hadn't even noticed Chris walk to stand beside her. Rachel opened her mouth, thinking of a way she could get out of it. It seemed clear to her that Chris had no idea of the history between her and Jack, and now was definitely not the time to share the sad story. She was sure that Jack would want her by his side exactly as much as he had wanted to be her instructor to jump out of a plane — and look how that had turned out.

'Great,' Chris said, his eyes fixed on the paramedics at work. 'I would go with him but then we would both be stranded at the hospital, which doesn't seem very sensible.'

Rachel opened her mouth to speak, but Chris had returned to his post by his friend's side. Rachel's mind briefly registered that this day could not get any worse: an ambulance trip with a bitter ex-boyfriend, who had been injured through her own fault, seemed as bad as it could get. Then she remembered that she had thought that already several times throughout the day, and maybe it was better not to tempt fate.

Jack was soon secured on the metal stretcher, and all those present stepped in to lift him off the ground. Rachel kept pace but slightly behind as they walked through the field of cows and back to the ambulance.

'Who's coming with us?' Greg said as he and his partner settled Jack onto the slightly more comfortable stretcher in the back of the ambulance.

'Er, that would be me,' Rachel said, holding up her hand a bit like a child in a school classroom.

'You don't sound very sure, love,' Greg joked before holding out a hand and helping her up the steps and into the back of the ambulance.

'You sit there.' He directed her to a seat that was just behind the driver and faced towards the back of the ambulance. Rachel did as she was told as she watched Greg hook Jack up to various monitors.

'How's the pain on a scale of one to ten?'

Jack's eyes found Rachel's, and she was sure he was glaring at her.

'Around an eight, I guess,' he said, obviously trying for nonchalance but failing. It was clear to anyone with eyes that he was in a lot of pain.

'Right, I'll get you something for that.'

Rachel watched as Greg busied himself with a locked cabinet set up at the top of the ambulance, pulling out a pre-packaged syringe.

'This should help with the pain, but might make you feel a little woozy.

The ambulance bounced along the uneven track and Rachel was flung from side to side, but the occasional moan from Jack made her hold back her complaints.

'Easy there, fella,' Greg said before glancing through the gap between the front seats. 'We're nearly on the main road. Then it should be smooth sailing.'

Rachel felt like her stomach was in a washing machine, jostled and spinning. She took slow, deep breaths and tried to focus on Jack. She watched as some of the tightness in his face seemed to relax and his breathing slowed a little. She glanced up at Greg, who nodded reassuringly.

'Rachel?' Jack asked, sounding a little sleepy.

Rachel leaned forward. 'I'm here. How are you feeling?'

'Better. That stuff's pretty good at taking the edge off.'

Rachel was sure it had done more than that, but it probably wasn't the time or place to point that out.

'Hey, are you okay?' Jack asked, and he twisted his head round to try and see her, not an easy task with a neck brace on. Greg reached out a restraining hand.

'Here, swap places with me,' Greg said standing up. Rachel followed his direction and sat in the chair, which could be twisted on the spot, and meant that she could sit down and see Jack.

'Right now I'm more worried about you,' Rachel said wondering if it was worth risking reaching out for his hand.

'I'm fine,' Jack said, in the way a person who has had one too many might sound. 'It's just a bum knee. Probably take me out for a season, but hey.'

Rachel felt all the guilt multiply within her. She had been so focused on what had happened that she had completely ignored the longer-term implications for Jack's career, which was both a job and a passion. She must have grimaced because Jack reached out for her hand.

'Don't look like that,' he said, giving her hand a squeeze. 'Come here,' he added, making a beckoning motion with his free hand. Rachel frowned, so he repeated the words and the action. With a quick look at Greg, who just grinned and shrugged, she leant forward so her face was closer to Jack's.

'It was totally worth it,' he said softly before closing his eyes. Rachel stayed where she was, wondering if he would say more. Not that he needed to; those words cut through all the guilt and the pain, and zeroed in on the part of her heart which she thought she had closed off forever.

'I've missed you, Rachel. I should never have . . . ' Jack's voice trailed off; his eyes were closed, and his face seemed to have lost the tight mask of pain.

'It kills pain and loosens tongues,' Greg said softly, without looking at Rachel. When she glanced at him, all his focus was on the large clipboard in his lap which he was filling in.

6

Rachel watched Jack for the rest of the journey as she tried to work out what the words meant and how she felt about them. He had said the words, the words that in the weeks and months after that fateful day she had longed to hear. She felt a flutter of hope that maybe they could find their way back together, but that was quickly extinguished by the part of herself that had grown armour to ward off the pain. You can't take what he has said as anything other than medication-induced rambling. Even if he had meant them at the time, they still meant nothing unless he really knew what he was saying.

The ambulance slowed, and she heard the sound of beeping as it reversed into a spot outside the Accident & Emergency Department. Greg opened the back doors and let down the steps before indicating that Rachel should step out. She did so, glad to be back in the fresh air, and watched as they unloaded Jack's stretcher. The movement seemed to bring him out of his doze, and his face turned pale as he tried to move into a more comfortable position. His eyes opened wide, and as he was wheeled past her, it was like he was seeing her for the first time.

'What are you doing here?' he asked indignantly, before yelping as the pain seemed to return in full force.

Rachel, not knowing what to do, stood in place. Should she follow? It seemed clear that Jack didn't want her there, but she also didn't think she should leave him alone. Once Chris got there, maybe she could leave.

'Follow me, love,' Greg's voice floated out of the doors which stood open. 'I'll show you a place you can wait.'

* * *

Rachel glanced at her watch, which was another reminder that she had left her bag containing her purse and her phone back at the Skydiving Club. Chris had rushed in to see her and asked for an update; and, when one wasn't forthcoming, had pestered several nurses until he was permitted behind the scenes. Rachel was stranded — even if she wanted to leave, she couldn't. She had no money, no cards, and no way to call someone to come and get her . . . and that was assuming she could convince herself that it would be an okay thing to do, which she knew it wasn't. She shifted in the hard plastic seat and sighed. The real problem was that there was nothing to distract her from thinking, and all she could think about was Jack.

Rachel had always hated airports, for obvious reasons, but there was another reason that she felt that way. The last time she had been in one was the last time she had seen Jack before today, and it was all such a tangled mess in her head. She could remember the look on his face and the pain that ran through her as she knew that it was over. She couldn't do what he was asking, and he had taken that as the ultimate rejection. And now she felt like she couldn't see straight, and somehow she had hurt him once more. Part of her knew that he must accept the risk of injury, if he was going to have a hobby like skydiving, but she also knew that experience mitigated some of those risks. If only she had paid more attention in the safety briefing; if only she had focused on Jack's words rather than the pet name he had for her that she hated. Well, maybe then she wouldn't be sat here in this waiting room, and he wouldn't be beyond the automatic doors with a potentially seriously injured knee and goodness knew what else.

Every time the automatic doors opened, Rachel sat up straighter and peered over the rows of chairs filled with an assortment of people to see who it was. One by one, names were called out, and groups of people disappeared through the doors. Occasionally the doors opened, and a person on crutches or with a freshly plastered arm walked out and headed towards the exit, with a mixed expression of shock and relief. Rachel felt both cold and a little stupid sat in the black-and-pink flight suit; not to mention that the curious glances of the other people waiting reminded her of the cows in the field. When Chris finally reappeared, Rachel was lost in a sea of miserable memories both distant and recent.

Chris took the spare seat beside her.

'Well, this wasn't exactly what I'd planned,' he said, his face set in a grim expression which didn't suit him.

'How's Jack?' Rachel asked, wondering if this was a sign of bad news.

Chris blew out a sigh and ran a hand through his hair.

'He has a fractured kneecap and probably ligament damage. They won't know until they get in there.'

Rachel could feel herself start to shake. She had known it wouldn't be great news — the amount of pain Jack had been in told her that there must be something seriously wrong — but what Chris had said seemed to be way worse.

'Hey, he's going to be okay,' Chris said, concerned, and pulled Rachel into a one-armed hug. 'I'm just glad you're okay, or this might have had to go down as the worst date I have ever organised — and let me tell you, there is some fierce competition.'

Rachel giggled. She knew that she shouldn't be laughing, but she also knew that in a few months' time this would quite possibly be a tale she used to regale her friends over a glass of wine. It was the most ridiculous and unlikely combination of circumstances ever.

'I'm going to head back to Jack's place to pick up some bits he's going to need, but I don't really want to leave him on his own. They reckon it's going to be a couple of hours before he goes into surgery. He won't admit it, but I know he's fretting, so would you mind waiting with him?'

Rachel tried not to stiffen in Chris's arms; she didn't want to give away any of her hidden feelings. It was clear that Jack hadn't told Chris about her, and she didn't want to make things any worse by blabbing out the whole story to him now. Chris was Jack's friend, Rachel reasoned, and so it was up to Jack to tell him if he wanted to. And anyway, Jack was probably out of it on painkillers, and wouldn't even know she was there.

'I'll pick up our things from the school as well, and then I can drop you back home whilst Jack's in surgery. They say it will take four hours at least.'

It was such a reasonable request, and since Rachel didn't want to explain the circumstances that could give her the only possible excuse not to accede, she had no choice.

'Of course,' Rachel said, and then

looked down. 'What about the jump-suit?'

'Well, you could take it off and sit here in your underwear?' Chris said with a twinkle in his eye. Rachel elbowed him, and he made a show of rubbing his supposedly sore ribs.

'I'll bring your clothes back so you can get changed. I can drop the suit back another day.' He leaned in and Rachel felt him kiss her gently on the top of the head. She closed her eyes. It seemed like forever since she had been held like that and told, without words, that she was important and that someone cared. Their first date had been an unmitigated disaster, that was for sure, but Chris had turned out to be a nice guy . . . and one she thought she wouldn't mind seeing again, maybe. Assuming that Jack didn't put him off by telling him about his experience with her. But what about Jack? A small part of her head — or was it her heart? — reminded her: Jack doesn't want you, he's told you that more than once.

How else do you want to hear it before you accept it — skywriting, maybe?

Jack had been moved to a ward full of men in traction or plaster, showing signs of having fallen off ladders and motorbikes, or involved in other sporting-related incidents. He was in and out of sleep, occasionally opening an eye. She felt sure he knew that she was there, but was either too tired to talk or simply didn't want to speak to her. Rachel wanted to tell him that she was sorry. She knew that she had played a part in the accident.

'It's okay,' Jack murmured sleepily

Rachel moved in a little closer so that she could hear what he was saying.

'I know you're sorry.'

Rachel's mind raced to replay the last few minutes. She hadn't said the words out loud, she was sure of it. She looked back to Jack, and there was that expression. The one she had loved, in the beginning, and which then at the end had annoyed her so. The expression that said he knew what she was thinking, but also knew that she couldn't find the way to say it out loud.

'Yes, well, it wasn't all my fault.' The words just sort of slipped out, and Rachel clamped a hand over her mouth to avoid any more truths escaping. Jack opened one eye again and fixed it firmly on her. Rachel tried to keep her face neutral, as she always did when she detected signs of an argument.

'Are you suggesting that any of this is my fault?' He always managed to sound so indignant and haughty.

'I know I wasn't doing what I was supposed to do, but there was no need for you to go all superhero and take the impact all on yourself.' Rachel knew that she shouldn't say it — she was arguing with a person who had been hurt trying to protect her — but somehow it still annoyed her. It was what he had always done: played the great protector and then made her feel bad when he got hurt, even when she had told him she didn't want him to do it in the first place.

'Well, maybe you should have just told Chris that you were afraid of heights — not to mention aeroplanes — rather than trying to impress him,' Jack hissed, trying to sit up a little and then going suddenly pale and reaching out for his leg. Rachel watched as he glared at her, as if him moving and causing himself pain was also her fault.

'You practically goaded me into it,' she hissed back, aware that others in the ward were now listening in.

'Aren't you the one who always said your mum's advice was best?'

Now it was Rachel's turn to glare.

Just because someone tells you to jump off a cliff, doesn't mean you should. It was a hurtful, if accurate, description of her mum. Jack had always gently teased her mother about her desire to keep both feet firmly on the ground, and Rachel had always found it charming, as had her parent. But now? Well, now it felt like he was using it to both hurt her and score points.

Jack was lying back on the pillow with his eyes squeezed shut.

'We don't need to talk about this,' Rachel said in what she hoped was a conciliatory manner. 'I am sorry that you got hurt, so let's just leave it at that.'

'Well, that's what you do best,' Jack mumbled. 'Leaving.'

Rachel opened her mouth; she wanted to explain, but knew that it was no use. She had tried to before and couldn't seem to make him understand, so why would now be any different? Instead, she held her peace, as she had done so many times before, and sat and waited for the nurse to come and wheel Jack into surgery.

7

When Chris arrived back on the ward where Rachel sat next to a space with no bed in it, she didn't think she had ever been so pleased to see someone. For starters, Chris smiled when he saw her; and that had to be better than being around Jack, who made his feelings about her eminently clear.

'How long's he been gone?' Chris asked as he handed her a cup of coffee, which she was relieved to note didn't come from the hospital cafeteria.

'About forty minutes,' Rachel said, not needing to look at her watch since she had done little but stare at the large wall clock opposite since Jack had been taken away. It was that or try to ignore the curious glances of the other patients, not to mention visitors on the ward.

'Right; well, in that case, I should

have time to take you home and return here before he's back on the ward.'

Rachel was about to suggest that Chris phone Jack's sister, Megan; but clamped her mouth shut, remembering that right now Chris didn't know that Jack and she had history, and she wanted to keep it that way.

'I've let his family know,' Chris continued, 'but his sister's away on business and can't get back till tomorrow, so I've said I'll hold the fort till then.'

'Look, I can get myself home. Why don't you stay here?' Whatever had passed between them, Rachel didn't like the idea that Jack might wake up from surgery alone.

'Don't be daft,' Chris said, and looked her full in the eye, 'Number one, it wouldn't be very gentlemanly of me to abandon you to public transport after a day like we've just had; and number two, I am literally the worst person at sitting still and waiting. Better to keep busy. I'll be back before he is;

and besides, they've got my number if they need anything in between.' Chris pulled his phone out of his pocket and waggled it.

'I brought your clothes if you want to get changed?' he added, looking from the bag he was carrying to the jumpsuit she was wearing — which Rachel knew looked ridiculous even when you were surrounded by other people wearing them, never mind when you were surrounded by folk dressed in normal clothes.

'Thanks,' Rachel said, grabbing the bag. 'I won't be a minute.'

Back in her own clothes and speeding along in Chris's car, Rachel could almost convince herself that nothing had happened; that they had been on a nice, normal date that hadn't started with her jumping out of a plane strapped to her ex-boyfriend's chest and then ended with him being wheeled into surgery. Chris also seemed to be a mind-reader, and had pulled off the motorway into the services and through a fast food drive-in. Rachel wasn't normally a big fan, but after the day she'd had, a greasy burger followed by salty fries and an apple pie was just what she needed, and she ate it all with gusto.

'Maybe I should have suggested that place as our first date?' Chris said, grinning as he picked up a french fry. 'You seem to enjoy it more than what I actually planned.'

Rachel felt herself go red, although whether at the fact that she had clearly not enjoyed something that Chris considered fun, like skydiving, or because she had consumed so much junk food in such a short space of time, she wasn't sure.

'Sorry,' she replied, not knowing what else to say.

'What for?' Chris asked, and he sounded surprised. 'For not liking jumping out of a plane? Rachel, lots of people wouldn't give it a go even if you paid them.'

Rachel turned to look at him, and her

radar registered his expression as genuine.

'You could have told me,' he added, and then frowned. 'Or maybe my friends are right and I should have paid more attention?'

Rachel smiled. Chris had a softer side and she suspected that was why Beth had thought they would make a good match.

'You're right, I should have told you.' Since Chris was still frowning, she reached out a hand and squeezed his arm. 'I guess I was just a bit embarrassed; you had clearly gone to a lot of effort, and I didn't want to ruin it.'

'Well, maybe next time you should pick?' Chris said.

Rachel thought about it for about a second.

'I'd like that, but I can't promise it will be as . . . ' Her voice trailed off as she searched for an appropriate word.

'Eventful?' Chris suggested.

'Eventful,' Rachel said with a smile.

* * *

Rachel closed her front door, and walked across the room to the window at the front of her studio flat. The tall, wide bay window was one of the reasons she had fallen in love with the place, even though it was impractically tiny. From the bottom of her bag she could hear her phone buzz; wondering if it was Chris, however unlikely that might seem, she reached in and read the screen. The sense of disappointment that it was Beth, her best friend, and not him, surprised her a little. Perhaps the date had been more successful than she thought.

'So . . . how did it go? Do you like him?' The phone hummed with Beth's excitement and anticipation.

'You won't believe the date I've just had.'

'That good, hey? Tell me all the details — and I mean all of them!'

Rachel settled herself in to the

shabby, sagging, two-seater sofa that ran the length of the one room she called home, and told Beth everything.

'So, how was it seeing Jack again?' Beth asked when Rachel finally finished.

'He got me so mad, I actually jumped out of a plane. How do you think it was?' Rachel replied. 'Then, because I was so terrified — ' Rachel winced at this, knowing that wasn't exactly the whole truth. ' — I forgot the instructions on what to do on landing, and now he's in hospital with a fractured kneecap. So I'd say it went about as well as our last meeting, wouldn't you?'

'But you didn't get hurt?' Beth asked, and Rachel knew that tone of voice. Anyone else might assume she was concerned for her friend's welfare, but Rachel knew better. When it came to romance, Beth was a traditionalist, and that meant her ultimate fantasy was being rescued by a handsome knight/ prince/hero.

'No,' Rachel said slowly. 'He did the hero thing, which I know you love, but then he got angry with me for making him have to rescue me. Which pretty much sums up the last few months of our relationship.'

'Well, I suspect when you go and visit him he will have calmed down a bit.'

'I don't think he wants me to visit, Beth. He made it very clear that he thinks it's my fault.' Rachel's mind went back to the ambulance journey and those words. The words she had wanted to hear since they had broken up. It's just the drugs, she told herself. Do not tell Beth; you'll never hear the end of it.

'Anyway,' Rachel said, deciding to move the conversation to safer grounds, 'don't you want to know how my actual date went with the actual guy you set me up with?'

'Don't tell me.' Beth sighed. 'He works in finance. Your views are poles apart, and you couldn't possibly . . . '

'We're going to go out again; and this

time, I'm going to pick the date activity.'

There was silence from the other end, and Rachel wondered for a moment if Beth had managed to accidentally hang up, as was her habit when she got excited.

'And there I was thinking that would get you all excited,' Rachel said sarcastically, wondering whether Beth was simply in shock that her blind date had been successful — in one area, at least.

'That's great,' Beth said, in a tone a person might use when their dentist announces they only need one filling.

Rachel stared out of the window, watching the next-door neighbour's cat parading up and down the low wall at the front of the terrace.

'You okay?' Rachel asked, not know-ing what else to say.

'Of course,' Beth said with forced cheerfulness. 'Just having trouble get-ting my head round all that's happened. I mean, that's some first date! I got distracted by the Jack factor, but now I'm all ears. Tell about Chris.' Beth was babbling as she usually did, but there was something forced about it. Rachel had known Beth since primary school, and she could just tell. 'Don't go all coy on me, now. I want details!'

Rachel shook off the feeling. She was tired. It had been an unbelievable rollercoaster of a day, and now she was projecting those feelings on to Beth.

'Well. He seems a genuinely nice guy. I mean, he talked about work a lot in the car, so I thought that was all there was to him, and you know how I feel about that kind of thing.'

Beth made a noise which Rachel took to mean she was listening.

'And then there was the whole skydiving thing, and the fact he seemed oblivious to the fact that I was terrified and it was literally the last thing I wanted to do . . . but then later he was really sweet and apologetic. He's obviously a good friend to Jack, although I wonder what he's done to deserve that. Anyway, we left it that we would get together again.'

'Did you set an actual date?' Beth asked.

'No, but he's gone back to the hospital to make sure he's there when Jack wakes up, so I guess he'll text me.'

'I'm sure he will,' Beth said brusquely. 'Anyway hon, I better go. My mum's cooking me dinner and you know how she gets when I'm late.' There was a short pause. 'Let me know when he texts.'

And then she was gone and Rachel was listening to the tone to say that she had been hung up on. Rachel stared at the phone and tried to work out if she was being over sensitive. Beth's reaction made no sense, which seemed to be evidence that it was all in Rachel's head. She swiped her thumb across the phone, just to check to see if she had any new messages. An act which was ridiculous in itself since she knew Chris would still be driving back to the hospital. Not knowing what else to do,

she padded across to her tiny kitchenette and put the kettle on to make a cup
of tea but making sure to take her
mobile with her.

8

When the phone rang and the familiar number appeared, Rachel pounced on it, gave Uncle Jeff an apologetic smile, and wove her way in between the stacks of cardboard boxes that lined the corridor which led to the small kitchen at the back of the shop. She took a deep breath and then pressed the button.

'Hi, Chris,' she said, thankful that he couldn't see the ridiculous grin that had spread across her face when she'd realised it was him who was calling.

'Rachel, hi.' He sounded distracted, which Rachel now knew meant he was at work. Unfortunately Chris was often at work when he called. He claimed to work days that were so long if he didn't call from the office, they would never speak. Rachel wasn't sure how she felt about this, but when she heard his voice she always forgave him, assuming there

70

was something for her to forgive.

'Listen, I know this is a bit cheeky, but I need a favour.'

Rachel felt a little glow start within her. When people, particularly those you had just started dating, asked you for a favour, it usually meant they trusted you. Either that or they were taking advantage, but Rachel knew that Chris didn't fit into that category.

'No problem,' Rachel said.

'You might want to wait and hear what it is before you volunteer,' he added.

'Well, as long as you don't want me to go skydiving again, I think we're good.'

There was a pause, and Rachel wasn't sure whether it was because Chris was distracted by something work-related, or if it was because he did in fact want her to jump out of a plane.

'Chris?'

There was the rustling of paper, and Rachel could hear the sound of fingers flying across a keyboard.

'Sorry. Trying to do too many things at once, which is kind of my problem.'

Rachel couldn't disagree with him there, but thought it was churlish to mention that in that moment.

'It's just — you know Jack is getting daily physio?'

'Uh-huh,' Rachel replied, her stomach sinking as she felt fairly sure she knew where this was going.

'Well, he's managed to get the last appointment of the day most days, so I can take him over there.'

'But?' Rachel said, knowing there had to be a 'but', and also knowing what Chris was going to ask her.

'He couldn't get an evening one today. I've tried to move the old work schedule around, but you wouldn't believe what's going on in the markets today, and there's no way I can get away to take him.'

'So you want me to take him.' She tried to keep the incredulousness from her voice. She knew, although she had never asked, that Jack must have told

Chris everything — from his perspective, of course. She had been pleasantly relieved that Chris had never brought up the subject.

'I've literally tried everyone else I can think of, but no go. I know it might be a bit awkward, but I've told Jack he will have to behave himself, and he's promised he will.'

Rachel groaned inwardly. Why did life have to be so complicated? Why did the new guy you just met have to be friends with your ex? Why? She frowned again as she remembered the conversation with Beth, who had insisted she'd had no idea and that it shouldn't matter, in that airy way she had.

'Look, if you really don't want to do it, I can arrange a taxi . . . ' Chris's voice trailed off. Since he had told her the last taxi guy had practically shut Jack's injured knee in the door, she knew she wasn't going to chance that happening again, whatever her complicated feelings were for Jack.

'Fine,' she said, this time not

bothering to hide her sigh, 'What time do I need to pick him up?'

'Four-thirty. You know the address?' Since Jack hadn't moved in the last five years, that seemed an obvious question.

'I owe you . . . ' Chris added, and she could hear that he was grinning.

'You do,' Rachel replied. 'Another date would be nice.' She would never have normally said anything so bold as that, but now seemed a good opportunity, so she went for it.

'You are right, of course. Work's been crazy, and with sorting Jack out . . . but yes. How about dinner? My treat?' There was the sound of keyboard-tapping at the other end of the phone. 'I should be able to get away on Friday, so shall we say dinner at eight? I'll swing by and pick you up at seven-thirty.'

'Sounds good,' Rachel said, as Uncle Jeff poked his head around the corner and made the face that told her she was pushing her luck, particularly since she was about to ask if she could leave early today. Jeff was a great guy and he had a real soft spot for her, but Rachel didn't like to take advantage of that fact.

'Got to go, bye,' she said, hanging up the phone. 'Sorry, it was important.'

Jeff nodded.

'It's about the guy who hurt himself at the weekend,' she added.

'So we're calling him *the guy*, are we?' Uncle Jeff said, heaving up a cardboard box and carrying it back through to the front of the shop. Rachel walked after him, knowing there was no way she could bluff her way out of it. Clearly someone had told him — probably Beth, who used to pop in regularly on her lunch break.

'There's nothing going on there,' Rachel said, knowing what his concerns would be.

'It's none of my business, of course, love, but I just don't want to see you get hurt like that again.'

Rachel peeled off the tape from the top of the cardboard box and started to unload the small tester pots of paint.

'Trust me, neither do I, and I'm only

going to see him to help out a friend.'
She used the word tentatively, since she
was wondering if she and Chris would
be more than friends, an idea that was
not without its appeal. Jeff looked at her
for a long time and Rachel smiled.

'It will be fine, really. Chris, the guy I
was actually on the date with, asked me
to take Jack to his physio appointment
today.'

Jeff nodded slowly, but it was clear he
hadn't been convinced.

'Relax, Uncle Jeff. Chris is taking me
out for dinner on Friday. I'm just
helping out. Jack and I could barely
manage to be civil last time I saw him.
It will be uncomfortable and awkward
for both of us, and then it will be over.'

Jeff disappeared for a moment and
then reappeared with another box.

'Just don't forget what happened
between you before, that's all I ask.'

Rachel leaned over and kissed him on
the cheek.

'I won't, I promise.' She gave him her
best *I need a favour* look.

'And no doubt you'll be needing to leave early in order to undertake this favour that will be both uncomfortable and awkward for you both.'

Rachel shrugged her shoulders helplessly.

'Thanks, Uncle Jeff. I'll make up the hours, I promise.'

* ★ *

Rachel had managed to squeeze her ancient Ford Fiesta into an impossibly small space. Unlike some other Londoners, she didn't have parking assist; instead, she had many years of practice of inching her way into tiny spaces or risking having to park miles away from where she wanted to be. The shop had no allocated parking, and so Rachel was used to the daily battle to snag one of the prime on-street spots — one that she prided herself on winning most days. That morning, she had managed the most sought-after space outside the little bakery, just four doors down from the hardware store. It was a prime spot because you could drive straight out as cars could only park behind.

Rachel glanced at her watch; she had left with plenty of time. If this encounter was going to be uncomfortable, she didn't want it to be because she was late picking Jack up.

Forty-two minutes later, and things weren't looking quite as rosy. Rachel had managed to travel just half a mile. As with all residents of London, she knew that she could have walked there faster. Having been stationary for most of this time, she decided to follow her fellow drivers and get out of the car to see if she could see what was happening.

A red double-decker bus was straddling both lanes. The boot was open and steam was issuing forth. The bus driver was standing on the pavement, talking into his mobile and trying to ignore the angry glares, comments and honking horns.

A woman dressed in black and

fluorescent yellow stepped from behind the bus, had a quick word with the driver, and then walked towards the line of traffic. She appeared to be directing the driver at the front of the queue to drive the wrong way down a one-way street which led off of the main road they were currently on.

When the police officer stepped beside her car, Rachel wound down the window.

'If you would like to follow the line of traffic, ma'am. My colleague is at the other end and he will direct you from there.'

'Thanks,' Rachel said, relief starting to mingle with hope that she might just make it. Pressing the left-hand indicator out of habit, she turned down the small side street, ignoring the white arrows which pointed firmly in the opposite direction. At the end of the street she could see the other police officer who was holding back traffic that clearly intended to use the side street correctly. To Rachel, it was like she could see the exit to a maze, and she put her foot down — being mindful not to break the speed limit in front of an officer of the law, however.

A flash of red appeared in front of her and Rachel stamped on the brakes. She felt her head lurch forward, and then she managed to brace herself against the impact, so that all she had to show for it was a red mark where her forehead had hit the steering wheel.

She rubbed at it and cursed the guy in the flashy red sports car who had pulled out of a hidden garage, even though technically speaking he was travelling in the right direction and she in the wrong. Judging by his expression and the gestures he was making with his hands, he was none too pleased.

The police officer ran towards them and hurriedly started to explain. The man in the flashy car was not so easily placated, as he gestured at her Fiesta, which had stopped mere inches from his prized automobile. Rachel drummed her fingers, all the while admiring the officer's patience, and waited whilst the other driver made a real drama out of reversing up the street. When Rachel finally reached the end, the officer tapped on the window.

'You alright, miss?' he asked, his eyes straying to the red mark the steering wheel had left.

'Yes, I'm fine, thanks,' Rachel said, forcing herself to smile reassuringly. He was only doing his job, but she didn't want him to start thinking he needed to get her checked out by medical personnel. She knew it was just a bump, and also knew what Jack's face would look like when she arrived late.

The officer nodded slowly, not entirely convinced, but was shaken from his thoughts by the sound of horns honking. He gave the driver behind Rachel a stern look, and then waved her on into the flowing traffic.

Rachel screeched to a halt outside the tall Victorian terrace that had been converted into modern and spacious flats, and risked a look up. True to form, there was Jack standing at the window, looking like she had just purposefully run him over with the car rather than merely being a little late. Rachel sighed as she reached across to grab her handbag. Uncomfortable and awkward it was, then.

9

Rachel pressed the doorbell for Jack's flat and could sense the impatience rolling off him through the closed door. It opened slowly as he tried to hop backwards with just one crutch and hold the door at the same time. He wobbled on the spot, and the only thing that Rachel thought could make this day worse was if he were to fall over and hurt himself further, and so she reached out an arm to steady him.

'Careful!' she said before he snatched his arm out of her grip, causing another period of unbalance. Rachel swallowed down the flash of anger but refused to step back. If he was going to be an idiot about her trying to help him, she wasn't just going to stand by and let his stubbornness cause him to fall down. Once he had restored his balance, he glared at her.

'Did you forget the time?' he asked icily as he reached for his other crutch.

'No,' Rachel said, trying to exhale the irritation she felt. 'There was a broken-down bus.'

'Huh,' he said, pocketing his door key. 'And I don't suppose that ever happens in London, does it?'

And with that he stalked past her, or at least tried to. Not an easy feat when you had one leg in a full-length splint that prevented any movement, and were trying to navigate a set of Victorian steps on a pair of crutches.

Rachel tried to mentally go to her happy place. She knew that if she responded in kind, however much she wanted to — and, quite frankly, felt she had the moral right to — it would only make things worse. His progress to the car, which Rachel had abandoned double-parked, was painfully slow and not appreciated by fellow road users, who had to take it in turns to bypass the obstruction.

Ignoring the horns and the colourful

language, Rachel counted to ten as Jack attempted to fold his six-foot frame into the passenger seat of her small, 'unsuitable for tall people' car, as he had always used to refer to it. His feelings towards it had no chance of softening as he jammed his injured leg under the dashboard before Rachel reached in and pushed the chair back as far as it would go. The angry colour had faded from his face, to be replaced by a pale sheen that told Rachel the process had hurt him, and she felt a flash of fresh guilt. She wanted to say something, but didn't know what, and so just hurried around and climbed in the other side.

'Right, where to?' Rachel asked, trying to ignore the flashing headlights of the van behind that were like lights at a rave.

'You don't know?' Jack asked.

Rachel took in a deep breath to try and calm her frazzled nerves. Obviously she didn't know, or she wouldn't be asking. It seemed pointless to reply, so she simply pulled away from the kerb and drove to the end of the road.

'You're going the wrong way,' was Jack's only comment.

'Which way would you like me to go?' Rachel asked, gripping the steering wheel so tightly that it made her forehead — which a glance in the rear-view mirror told her was still red — throb.

'Head for the South Circular. Physio's in Bromley.' Jack started to rub at his leg as if he felt he needed to remind her that he was the injured party. Either that or his leg just hurt, she thought, trying to be the bigger person.

The directions were the only form of conversation. Jack did not appear to want to talk about anything else, and by the time Rachel had navigated her way to the South Circular during rush hour, she wasn't feeling so chatty either. With an imperious gesture, Rachel was directed to pull in behind a low, squat building that advertised a Sports Physiotherapy business, which thankfully had a car park. Jack glanced at his watch.

'Are we late?' Rachel asked, knowing that was what she was supposed to say, and not sure she could cope with any more drama if he took offence at her not asking.

'No,' Jack conceded, albeit reluctantly.

'Good.' Rachel said, and allowed herself a self-satisfied smile as she hopped out of the car and walked around to open his door for him. If it was a struggle to get him into the car, it was a battle to get him out. By the time Jack was upright, he was running with sweat and taking in harsh breaths through his teeth. He went to walk, but Rachel placed a hand firmly on his chest.

'Easy there, tiger. Take a minute to get your breath back.'

Rachel wondered if he would argue, but he didn't seem to have the energy. The side door to the practice swung open, and a woman about the same age as Rachel stepped out, dressed in tracksuit bottoms and an aertex shirt that advertised the business. She held out a hand to Rachel and smiled.

'Hi, I'm Jen. You must be Rachel.'

Rachel's returning smile faltered just a little as she imagined just what Jack had been saying about her.

'Yes, that's me,' Rachel said, going for cheerful acknowledgement but also risking a glance at Jack, who seemed to be concentrating on his breathing a little too hard.

'Right, Jack. You know what we physios like to say at moments like this.' Jen had turned her attention to Jack, and was still smiling, although Rachel thought she could detect some concern.

'No pain, no gain,' Jack hissed through his clenched teeth before he started hopping towards the door.

Rachel followed behind Jen, who was studying Jack's gait as he moved into the reception area.

'We're in the main gym,' she said, and led the way to a set of double doors that she held open for Jack. Rachel stopped and looked at the reception area that contained a couple of chairs and a few dog-eared magazines. It looked like a suitable place to wait and fantasise about what she was going to do with the rest of her evening, when she would be free of her angry, petulant passenger.

'Come on through,' Jen said. 'I have a suspicion that Jack hasn't been doing his exercises, and I might need a comrade to do the nagging.'

Rachel opened her mouth to point out that she was the last person who Jack would want either in the room or to nag him. She still felt guilty as well, and seeing Jack struggle and in pain did not help those feelings, even though she knew that it was not entirely her fault that he had been hurt. She wanted to stay where she was, but Jen was having none of it, standing at her post by the door. So Rachel fixed a smile on her face which told the world it wasn't the worst idea ever, and walked into the gym.

There were several other physios working out with people, who to Rachel all looked like professional sportsmen and -women. Rachel was directed to a set of school-assembly-type chairs along one wall, and watched as Jack heaved himself up on a padded bench so that Jen could remove his splint. Jen ran practised hands over Jack's knee before starting to test how far he could bend it.

'Have you been doing your exercises?' Jen asked, focused on her task.

Rachel could see the answer on Jack's face. She'd know that look anywhere. It was almost childlike, speaking of being caught out but unsurprised.

'I'll take that as a no,' Jen said as she reached for an ice pack before strapping it around his knee. Jack winced.

'Jack, I don't need to tell you that we are on a tight schedule here. If you want to be competition-fit by the start of the season, then you need to put in the work.'

'I've been thinking about that. I don't think it's a realistic goal,' Jack said, refusing to make eye contact and focusing on his knee.

'And I've told you it's not impossible, but I can't be the only one putting in the work.' Jen was standing with her arms crossed, waiting for Jack to look at her. 'And you know all this. I've talked at length with your consultant, and he has signed off on the treatment plan. If I go back to him and report your progress, he's going to have the same concerns I have.'

Jack looked up now.

'I can't imagine he's going to be overly concerned if I have to miss the start of the season, unless he's a betting man.'

Jen said nothing for a couple of heartbeats, her face never changing from its determined expression.

'He agrees with me, Jack. If you don't put the work in now, there won't *be* any more seasons.'

Jack stared at Jen, and Rachel stared

at both of them. Jack seemed to be waiting for Jen to say something else. Jen seemed to think she had said all she needed to.

'Fine,' Jack said. 'Whatever. I'll just go back to the NHS physio and hope they can get me to the point where I can walk without a limp.'

He swung his legs to the ground and grabbed for the splint. Rachel knew she couldn't sit by and watch this performance any longer. Even if Jack was prepared to give up, she knew she wasn't. She had almost stood in his way before, and she wasn't about to let that happen again, especially since it was her fault that Jack was here.

'I never figured you for a quitter.' Rachel tossed the words out, knowing they were a challenge.

'I never fractured my knee and tore several ligaments before,' Jack spat back.

Rachel tilted her head to one side. 'Oh, please. You've had plenty of injuries, plenty of challenges you've overcome in the past. Surfing is not just your life, it's your career. And now you're prepared to throw away all that hard work, all that pain, because you don't feel like doing your exercises?'

'You're one to talk.' Jack was glaring at her now, but at least he was paying attention. 'You've never stood up to a challenge in your life. What's your motto? Don't bother climbing a mountain when you can just walk round it?'

It was a low blow, even if there was an element of truth in it. Jen was watching the argument like a tennis fan, her head moving from one side to the other.

'What would your folks say?' Rachel asked, more softly this time. He wasn't the only one to resort to low blows.

His face coloured, and she could see him clench his fists as he seemed to battle with a force inside him.

'Don't you dare,' he said finally, breathing heavily, 'You have no right to bring them into this. Especially this. Every time you come into my life, you bring pain and disaster.' Jack had forced himself to his feet, and was now standing toe-to-toe with Rachel.

Rachel looked up into his furious face.

'That's more like it,' she said. 'Get mad, hate me if you need to. Do whatever you need to, but don't you dare give up.'

Jack's face relaxed just a little.

'Why do you care? After this, you can go back to your life completely unaffected by your actions, once again.'

The words stung, and Rachel lifted a hand to her cheek; she almost felt as if he had physically struck her.

'So why don't you just go now?' Jack continued. 'I can make my own way home, and I'd be a lot happier with you out of my life.'

Rachel knew what she needed to do, if she was ever going to be able to forgive herself for her part in this, both past and present. She looked at Jen and nodded in answer to the silent question.

'Because I am going to get your lazy

butt competition-ready if it's the last thing I do.' Rachel's eyes flared with the challenge, 'And the quicker you get there, the quicker you can get me out of your life.'

10

Jack had scowled and winced his way through his workout, but at least he had done it. Every time he looked like he wasn't giving one hundred percent, Rachel had merely raised an eyebrow, and the silent challenge was laid before him. By the time Jen had ended the session, Jack was bathed in sweat, but had managed to meet the physio's demands.

'Great, same time tomorrow,' Jen said cheerfully, completely ignoring Jack's glowering face. 'And remember to do your exercises first thing and at lunchtime. Do you need another printout?' she asked innocently, as if to suggest that that was the reason Jack wasn't keeping up his end of the bargain.

'No,' Jack said stiffly as Jen strapped his knee back into the full-length splint.

He moved forward off the bench and gingerly found his feet. Jen stood back and watched, and it was clear that she expected him to do that without assistance.

'Off you go, then,' Jen said as she exchanged a quick grin with Rachel. 'Have you got the exercise sheet?' She directed this question at Rachel, who waved the printed sheet at her, even though they both knew she had it since Jen had printed it off not five minutes before.

Jack's posture suggested he was ignoring them, and he moved with remarkable speed towards the double doors before pausing, clearly waiting for one of them to open them for him. Rachel took her time, but made her way across the hall and pulled a door open.

'Thanks Jen, see you tomorrow.'

Jack hopped on a couple of paces and then paused.

'Chris is bringing me tomorrow,' he said, and Rachel was sure she could sense a slight panic in his voice;

although whether it was because she had become his self-appointed taskmaster or he simply didn't want to spend any more time with her, Rachel wasn't sure. She also knew that she didn't care.

'Well, I will be ringing him and telling him that I will be taking over. He's struggling to escape from work, so I don't expect he will mind.'

Jack stared, clearly unhappy with the new arrangement; but his shoulders seemed to sag a little, giving the message that he knew arguing would be a waste of time.

She was going to do this. She was going to get Jack back fit, and then she was going to move on with her life, possibly with Chris. An image of Chris floated into her mind, and she smiled.

'Are you going to stand their grinning like a loony, or get me home so I can take some pain relief?'

It was such a childish statement, but Rachel could see from Jack's face that he was probably being honest about his need for some analgesia, so she pushed the image of Chris from her thoughts and hurried out the door in front of Jack to open the car.

The car journey back to Jack's flat started off in stony silence. Rachel refused to be infected by Jack's mood. He had made progress today; and Jen had reassured her that, if he worked hard enough, he would fully recover. Rachel was going to see to it that he did, whether he liked it or not.

Jack refused to look at her, and so to fill the silence as the crawled along in the rush-hour traffic, Rachel switched on the radio and started to sing along.

When they reached Jack's flat, they had to repeat their earlier performance, with Rachel's car blocking one lane and Londoners sharing their thoughts on the inconvenience. Rachel was used to this, and ignored them as she walked behind Jack up the steps to make sure he got indoors in one piece.

'Right, I'll be here at five tomorrow.

Should give us plenty of time to get to your appointment.'

Jack nodded, and opened his mouth as if he was going to say something, but then thought better of it.

'And I'll ring you before work — about seven-thirty — to check you have done your morning exercises?'

'If you make it eight, I might actually answer.' Jack's tone was full of forced grumpiness, but Rachel was sure she could detect a slight thawing of relations.

'Eight it is, then. Talk to you tomorrow.' She smiled; Jack did a kind of half-smile, half-shrug; and then Rachel ran down the steps, waving a cheery hand at the latest car-driving horn-blower, and drove off in the direction of home.

The next morning, Rachel had her key in the lock of the back door to the hardware shop when her phone started to vibrate and squeak as if it were a mouse just noticing a cat. She stepped through the door and threw the deadbolt back into place before dropping her bag on the floor and fishing her mobile out of her jeans pocket. The reminder on her phone flashed *8am nag*; not that she needed the note to remind her what it was for. A quick glance at her wristwatch confirmed the time; she scrolled though her contacts until she found Jack's number — a number that she had never quite managed to bring herself to delete — and pressed the green phone symbol.

The phone rang five times, and Rachel frowned, wondering if Jack would be childish enough to ignore her call, since he knew exactly when she was going to ring and why. Mentally, she started rehearsing a sternly-worded answerphone message along the lines of 'Don't make me drive round there . . . '

The phone beeped and a breathless voice said, 'Hello?'

'Are you alright?' Rachel asked, crossness fast disappearing as her mind started to conjure up all sorts of images of Jack in trouble.

'Of course,' he said gruffly. 'I'm just doing as my commandant demanded.'

Rachel ignored the insult; at least he was doing what he needed to do. It didn't matter what he felt about her — surely their relationship couldn't deteriorate any further. All that mattered was the he got back to his best, and then she could finally move on.

'Well, good. I haven't really got time to drive round and stand over you whilst you do them.' Rachel knew she shouldn't have bitten, but there was something about the way that Jack spoke to her that wound her up.

'I hear you have another date with Chris on Friday,' Jack said, which seemed an out-of-the-blue question to Rachel.

'Yes,' she answered, working at keeping her voice neutral. After all, why shouldn't she have another date with Chris? Not that it was any of Jack's business!

There was silence from the other

end, and Rachel did nothing to fill it. She wasn't about to share details, or check that Jack was alright with her dating one of his friends.

'He's a good mate . . . ' Jack started, and Rachel could feel one of her eyebrows rise. What exactly was he insinuating?

'Well, I like him,' she replied frostily.

There was another pause, and Rachel had a sudden desire to hang up and finish this massively awkward conversation.

'He seems to like you,' Jack said tonelessly.

On the other end of the phone, Rachel could feel herself blush; although whether it was the thought that Chris had told Jack that he liked her, or because her ex was the first to tell her that, she wasn't sure.

'Just . . . just be careful, Rachel.'

Rachel held her phone away from her ear so that she could glare at it. Had Jack really just warned her not to hurt Chris?

'You just said Chris is a good mate, so why would you be worried that he would hurt me?' Rachel replied, deliberately interpreting his words differently to what she was sure he'd intended.

'Sometimes we don't mean to, but we do,' Jack said.

'Since Chris is a grown man, I'm sure he will be able to look after himself.' Rachel couldn't believe that they were actually having this conversation, and in that moment she knew she was going to stop it. 'Anyway, I've got a shop to open, so I'd better go. I'll call back at lunchtime to check you've done your second set of exercises, and pick you up at five.' Rachel spoke without a pause so as not to give Jack a chance to utter another word.

'Bye,' she said, trying to force some cheerfulness into her voice. The best way to cope with this, she decided, was to pretend the conversation had never happened. She would go back to being detached and cheerful, encouraging

Jack but from a distance, and Jack would . . . well, Jack was going to do whatever he was going to do.

11

Rachel risked another glance at her watch. If things didn't move along, she was going to barely have enough time to get changed when she got in, let alone have a shower and put some makeup on.

'Am I keeping you from something?' Jack said through gritted teeth as he navigated his way between two horizontal poles like the double bars in gymnastics. Rachel looked up, ready to point out that he knew exactly what she was running late for and there was no need to be snide about it, when she caught sight of his pale face which was beaded with the sweat of hard work and pain. With a deep breath, Rachel held her tongue, and simply smiled.

'Sorry, my last appointment over ran a bit,' Jen said, and gave Rachel a small conspiratorial smile. Rachel had no idea how much Jen knew about her history with Jack — she had certainly not told her any of the details — but she suspected that if Jen were to guess, she wouldn't be far off the mark.

'Watch the angle of your knee and the placement of your foot,' Jen said, immediately swapping back to professional mode. 'You need your muscles aligned if we are going to strengthen them.'

Rachel watched as Jen knelt down and repositioned Jack's foot, causing a wince of discomfort.

'At least I can see the new regime is working.' Jen said, looking up at Rachel briefly before switching her concentration back to the job in hand.

'Hmm,' Rachel murmured. 'Clearly my promise that he would never have to see me again once he was match-fit did the trick.'

Jack's step faltered and his knee seemed to crumple beneath him. Jen, always alert to this possibility, was behind him, supporting his weight until he found his balance again.

'That would seem to be a sign that you've had enough for one day.'

'I'm fine.' Jack's voice sounded hollow and strained.

Jen laughed. 'Oh, that's right. Yesterday I couldn't get you to do anything, but today I can't seem to stop you from potentially overdoing it.'

Rachel couldn't be sure, but she thought Jack whispered, 'Women!' under his breath. However, he allowed Jen to lead him back to the physio couch so she could replace his splint.

'Don't go back the other way. Just because you're not seeing me over the weekend doesn't mean I don't expect you to show signs of all the exercise work you are going to do.'

'As if I'd dare,' Jack said, and Rachel looked up sharply. This wasn't said in his now-familiar sullen tone: it was almost, but not quite, said in amusement. She blinked; she had forgotten that Jack even had a sense of humour.

'Come along, then, hopalong,' Rachel

said, knowing she was risking a return to sharp words but Jack peered up at her through his damp fringe and almost smiled. He pulled himself up onto his crutches.

'Well, I know how much you hate to be late.' It was another dig, Rachel knew it; but this time it was said more softly, like he used to. Rachel smiled uncertainly, not sure what to make of this sudden change in attitude, and led the way out to the car.

When they got back to Jack's flat, he insisted that she just drop him off rather than performing her previous role of shepherding him up the steps and seeing him safely in his front door.

Rachel was still frowning when she finally found a parking spot near her home. A glance at the dashboard clock told her that she had exactly twenty-two minutes before Chris's arrival; so, pushing Jack from her mind, she raced for her front door.

Considering the minimal time she'd had, Rachel had to allow herself to be a little impressed. She had dried and straightened her hair, which was now lying silky-smooth across her shoulders. She had gone for light makeup and her 'second date' evening outfit that consisted of a long black cotton dress that reached her ankles and her red ballet pumps. To finish off the effect, she had gone for a chunky silver necklace and a black bolero with a little sparkle. It was an outfit that she always thought could take her anywhere: not too over the top for a pub, and you could also get away with it in a reasonably posh restaurant. After their first date, Rachel had no idea where they were going, but figured this was her best 'anywhere' outfit — unless, of course, date number two involved some form of extreme sport.

A beep from outside tore her gaze away from the mirror that hung beside her front door, the flat being so small there really was nowhere else to hang it. She didn't bother to glance out the window, but grabbed her keys and bag and headed out.

Rachel couldn't keep from grinning. Despite the overwhelming failure of their first date, she had at least decided that she quite liked Chris, and would be happy to explore their relationship in a second date. Holding onto her skirts, she ran down the steps and pulled open the car door, ducking down just to check it was Chris. When she saw his face grinning at her, she smiled and climbed in beside him.

'Rachel, hi!' he said, with an enthusiasm which was not lost on her, and made the warm glow inside her flare just a little.

'How are you?' he asked, before leaning over and giving her a peck on the check.

'Good, thanks,' Rachel said, knowing that the kiss had brought a little colour to her cheeks and cherishing how good that felt.

'So, after our last date, I thought I'd play it safe and we would go for dinner somewhere nice.'

'Perfect,' Rachel said, and then

giggled. Chris took his eyes off the road for a moment, looked at her, and then turned his attention back to concentrate on driving.

'Do I take it that I am now fodder for gossipy sessions with your girlfriends?'

Rachel looked at him as he raised an eyebrow, but could see a smile ghost across his face.

'Maybe,' she said. 'But to be honest, I'd be more interested in hearing about the other date.'

'What other date?'

'The one that was worse than taking the woman who is terrified of flying skydiving? You said that wasn't even your worst date ever.'

'Ah,' Chris said. 'I was kind of hoping you had forgotten about that. I'm not sure it shows me in the best light.'

'Those are the best kinds of stories. Definitely second-date material.'

Chris sighed. 'Very well, then, but no judgement until you've heard it all.'

By the time they had reached their destination, Rachel was laughing so hard she had to hold her sides from the pain.

'That's terrible!'

'I know,' Chris said ruefully as he pulled the keys from the ignition and got out of the car. Rachel followed suit — not easy, as she was attacked by another wave of giggles.

'That's not the worse part,' he said as he walked around to stand beside her.

'There's more?!'

'The camel bit her.'

Rachel stared at him and then burst into loud hysterical laughter. Fighting for breath, she said, 'So having been through all that, she was then bitten by the camel?'

Chris ran a hand through his hair and looked rueful. 'Yep. Thankfully she didn't need stitches, but she did have to get a tetanus booster.'

Rachel thought she was going to have to sit down, and was briefly glad that she had chosen to wear waterproof mascara as she could feel a tear escape and run down her face.

'Well, one thing's for sure: I feel lucky that all you wanted me to do was jump out of a plane!'

Chris looked pained for a minute, and then joined in with Rachel as she laughed some more.

'Now, that *is* a story to share with my girlfriends!'

'I'm just glad that this time I've managed to make you laugh. At least tonight you look like you are enjoying yourself. Makes a change from the gut-wrenching terror you wore through most of our last date.'

Rachel nudged him with her elbow as the stepped through the door into an Italian restaurant and were greeted by a maître d' in full penguin-suit glory.

'Table for Chadwick,' Chris said, still grinning at Rachel.

'Ah yes, sir. You'll be pleased to know your other guest has arrived.'

Rachel looked from the maître d' to Chris — who did not seem surprised by this news — to the restaurant. A raised hand waved at her, and it was not who she was expecting. Not that she *had* been expecting anyone else — this was, after all, a date.

12

'Hi Chris!' Beth said enthusiastically as Rachel and Chris made their way over to the table, which had clearly been laid for three.

Rachel couldn't do much but stare as Chris and Beth exchanged the Italian greeting of kissing each other on both cheeks.

'Beth?' Rachel asked when they had finished, hoping that her best friend would pick up on all the hidden questions in that simple hello.

Beth giggled and pulled Rachel into a full hug.

'I thought you might need back-up,' Beth said quietly.

Rachel frowned. 'On a date?' she whispered back.

'Well, the last one wasn't exactly a resounding success,' Beth murmured before letting her friend go so that they could all sit down. Rachel's face still wore a *What on earth is going on?* expression.

'Ignore her,' Chris said, waving over the waiter. 'She was moaning that it was Friday night and she had nothing to do. She practically begged to come.'

Beth glared at him, and Chris stuck his tongue out in return.

'A bottle of champagne, please,' Chris said to the waiter, who nodded his head and faded away as all good waiters do.

Rachel was trying to process it all, not least the champagne, as she wondered if they had something to celebrate . . . other than her surviving jumping out of a plane.

'Anyway, since she set us up,' Chris said, directing his comment towards Rachel, 'and clearly persuaded you that I was worth a second chance, I thought it was the least I could do.'

Rachel allowed herself a little smile. It was not what she expected on a second date, but it was kind of sweet that he didn't want a friend to be home alone and miserable. She would still have words with Beth later, though. Crashing a date? Beth should know better!

The champagne arrived, and the waiter poured them each a glass.

'To Beth,' Chris said, raising a glass, and the women followed suit. They all took a sip. 'And to Rachel, for being brave enough to risk going out with me again — particularly after hearing the camel story.'

Beth snorted; it would seem she had heard that story before. They all toasted and took another sip.

'Right,' Chris said. 'Let's order food before we catch up. I'm starving.'

'So how was Jack today?' Beth asked as soon as they had given their orders. Rachel mentally rolled her eyes. It was one thing to have Beth along on her date to act as some kind of old-fashioned chaperone; it was another to move the topic of conversation to Rachel's ex-boyfriend.

'His usual cheerful self,' Rachel said; then, feeling that was a bit mean, 'He's making progress. Jen, his physio, says he should be back to competing by the start of the season.' Rachel took a sip of champagne in the hope that would be the end of the subject. 'So, Chris, how was your day?' she added, unable to think of another safe topic.

Chris opened his mouth to speak, but Beth started to talk before he could. 'When does the season start?' she asked.

Chris looked at Beth and then at Rachel, and Rachel thought she could detect a trace of regret at his impulsive invitation.

'September time. Australia is the first big comp. Jack should be out there at the end of August to start acclimatisation.'

The waiter arrived then, placing steaming bowls of pasta in front of each of them, and offering round the plate of garlic bread before leaving it in the centre of the table. They all dived in.

'So, Rachel, you said you were studying for a Master's, but you never told me what in?' Chris looked at Rachel and grinned. Rachel giggled and leaned over with her napkin to wipe off the trail of spaghetti sauce that was running down his chin. Chris smiled back.

'Do you think you'll get to go out and visit him this year?' Beth interrupted. Rachel clenched her hands in her lap and had to take a deep breath to avoid the urge to kick her friend under the table. What exactly was she doing? Why was she so obsessed with bringing the conversation back to Jack at every turn? One look at Chris told Rachel that she wasn't the only one who was uncomfortable with this line of questioning.

'Doubt I'll be able to get the time off,' Chris said hurriedly, and then turned his gaze to Rachel, his smile tight and his eyes almost pleading for forgiveness. Rachel reached out and squeezed his hand under the table to tell him it was alright. She was best friends with Beth, and so knew her lack of awareness of awkward conversation of old.

'Ethnology,' Rachel said quickly, before Beth could get in another inappropriate question.

Chris raised an eyebrow.

'I've no idea what that is,' he admitted, and Rachel laughed.

'You're not the only one, trust me,' said Beth; who, for now at least, seemed happy for Rachel to talk about herself and not Jack.

'Essentially, I look at the folklore of different ethnicities.'

Chris nodded, and Rachel felt she had his full attention.

'Right . . . ' he said, and then grinned, clearly still not sure what Rachel was going on about.

Rachel smiled. That was often the reaction she got.

'So, at the moment I am looking at the oral customs of different cultures. The stories they tell each generation, and where these stories come from.'

Chris nodded and waved a hand to indicate he was listening.

'Some cultures tell stories merely for entertainment, some to allow successive generations to remember the history of those that have gone before, and still others to instil cultural mores in the younger generations.'

'Like the early fairy tales?' Chris asked.

Rachel sat back in her seat; she couldn't help but be impressed that Chris had made the connection.

'What?' he said in mock hurt. 'Just because I work in the boring world of finance doesn't mean that I'm a philistine.'

'Most people ask her what she is going to do with the qualification when she's finished,' Beth said, keeping her eyes focused on the plate in front of her. Rachel blinked. Beth's tone had been neutral, but she knew her friend well enough to recognise a dig when she heard one. She could feel tears prick at the edges of her eyes. Why was Beth behaving like this? Attacking Rachel in front of the man she had said was perfect for her?

'I've always admired people who study something they love,' Chris said, breaking the now-awkward silence. Rachel flashed Chris a grateful smile. She then risked a look at Beth, who at least had the grace to blush.

The rest of the meal passed in a less eventful fashion. In fact, when Chris asked for the bill, Rachel was beginning to wonder if she had imagined the earlier events. Beth seemed to have returned to her usual funny, best-friend-type personality, and they had all shared laughs and stories, none of which involved Jack.

'We'll walk you to your car, Beth. Where did you park?' Chris asked as they were handed their coats by the maître d'.

'I got a taxi,' Beth said airily. 'I figured you wouldn't mind dropping me home.' She smiled and then stepped out of the door, leaving Chris looking somewhat helpless.

'I could offer to pay,' Chris said apologetically. 'For the taxi, I mean.' As if Rachel needed clarification.

'At this time on a Friday night, if she hasn't booked one she'll have to wait hours,' Rachel said as her mind tried to work out exactly what Beth was playing at. It was so unlike her, Rachel felt sure something must be wrong.

'I'm sorry,' Chris said, appearing unwilling to step out of the door after Beth. 'I'm starting to feel like this date wasn't much better than the last one.'

Rachel slipped her arm through Chris's.

'It's fine; she's my friend too, remember. Something's up with her. No doubt she'll tell me later.' She grinned up at him to try and reassure him, 'And since no camels or planes were involved in this date, I think we should mark it off as a success, even if we did end up with a chaperone!'

They stepped through the door arm in arm to find Beth waiting somewhat impatiently, particularly since she was cadging a lift.

'Come on, you two!' she said, walking off in the direction of Chris's car. 'Are you alright in the back, Rachel? You know the London traffic makes me carsick.'

Rachel sighed, and climbed in behind the front seat, which Beth had pulled forward for her. There really was no way to elegantly slip into the back seat of a three-door.

'If you drop Rachel off first . . . ' Beth said, sliding into the front beside Chris. Chris opened his mouth to speak, but Beth continued, 'I live further away, so it makes sense.'

Rachel tried not to glower at the back of her friend's head. What was she playing at? She had hoped for a goodnight kiss, but couldn't see that happening now. For someone who had thought Rachel needed to get out and date again, and that Chris was a perfect

match . . . well, Beth had a funny way
of showing it.

13

Rachel stepped through her front door and tried to calculate how long it would take Chris to drop Beth home in the quiet traffic. She wanted to speak to Beth, but didn't want to risk the embarrassment of having her still be with Chris when she did so. Something was definitely up, and Rachel was determined to find out what.

She picked up her phone and Googled the route to give herself something to do as she paced up and down. Her phone complied with the request, and an electronic 'ping' told her that in current traffic conditions it would take nineteen minutes. Rachel glanced at her watch and decided she would allow thirty, just to be sure.

As she watched the minutes drag by, she thought about Chris; and decided that, if he suggested it, she would say yes to a third date. She couldn't remember the last time she had felt so relaxed in someone else's company. Not exactly true, a voice said in her head; she had felt like that about Jack once. Rachel shook her head as if to get rid of the memories that threatened, and turned her attention to her phone.

It rang and rang, and then Beth's voice clicked in. 'Sorry, I can't take your call at the moment. You know me, only a serious emergency would take me away from my mobile, so leave a message after the tone and I'll get back to you once the crisis has passed.'

Rachel frowned. Beth's message was right; she always answered the phone. Even in places that Rachel would have been too embarrassed to do so, like hospitals where big signs gave dire warnings of what could happen if you did, Beth just laughed it off.

'Beth? It's me, Rachel. Are you okay? Look, I know something's going on with you. Best friends, remember?' Rachel wasn't sure why she needed to point that out, but after the confusing evening it seemed wise to remind her, just in case she had forgotten. 'Call me? I'm worried about you.' That last comment should do it. Beth would ring back as soon as she got the message.

Only she didn't. By lunchtime the following day, Rachel was obsessively checking her phone, even managing to ignore the disapproving tuts from Uncle Jeff, who thought the invention of mobiles was the end of civilised society. She had left four more messages, but still heard nothing, and now she was officially worried.

'If you are that concerned, pet, maybe you should pop over to see her in your lunch break.'

Rachel was startled from her latest study of her phone by his voice, and she blushed with embarrassment. She knew that she wasn't particularly focused on the job in hand. Uncle Jeff did pay her to work, after all, and now he was offering to let her have an extended lunch break. Beth worked in central

London, so it would take a good hour and half to make it there and back on the bus. But something was up with her, Rachel was sure.

'Maybe she's just lost her phone or turned it off?' Uncle Jeff's voice cut through Rachel's distraction. She laughed. Beth never turned her phone off, not even in the cinema, much to the annoyance of other patrons. Her phone beeped, and with an apologetic grin she turned it on.

You OK? the message read; only it wasn't from Beth, it was from Jack. Rachel frowned, wondering if he could psychically pick up on her mood. When they had been together she had always felt they were in tune, even if they were separated by miles.

Fine. Why? she typed back before she could allow herself to read too much into it.

I didn't get my morning nag came the reply, and Rachel felt the urge to slap herself on the forehead. She had been so distracted by worrying about

Beth that she had managed to completely forget about Jack.

Sorry, she texted. *Trying to get hold of Beth and no reply. Worried.* She didn't want to describe to Jack the whole second-date debacle, but she needed to share her concern with someone, Jack and Beth had gotten quite close during the time she and Jack had been an item.

She's fine. Texted me this morning.

Once again Rachel was left staring at her phone. Beth had texted Jack, whose number she had sworn she had permanently deleted in solidarity with Rachel's broken heart, but not answered any of her increasingly concerned messages? Rachel recalled the events of the previous night and tried to work out if she had upset Beth. She quickly threw out that idea. If you upset, Beth you knew about it; she wasn't one to sulk.

You sure you're OK? Jack added, and a little something inside Rachel seemed to blossom. It's just a reminder, she told herself firmly, of how things used to be. Don't read anything in to it.

I am now. Thanks for the update. Now stop texting me and get on with those exercises. I'll be there at 5 sharp to pick you up.

There, that was matter-of-fact, and couldn't give away how his show of concern had made her feel. The last thing Rachel needed right now was complications with her ex.

Rachel became aware that there were customers in the shop and a small queue had formed at the till. She put her phone back in her pocket. She might not have spoken to Beth, and there was still something strange going on, but at least she knew she was okay. Uncle Jeff glanced at her, and she knew that he would never openly complain but that he really needed her to do her job right now, so she stepped towards the counter briskly and asked, 'Who's next, please?'

The day was a busy one, and meant that Rachel hadn't much time to ponder what was going on with Beth. Her phone had remained resolutely silent, but Rachel had made up her mind. After she had dropped Jack back home she would drive round to Beth's. Beth might be able to ignore her phone calls and texts, but she would be hard pushed to ignore the sight of Rachel standing on her doorstep ringing the bell.

She arrived in Jack's street with five minutes to spare, and was surprised to see him standing at the bottom of the steps to his flat. He smiled as she pulled up at the kerb, and Rachel had the feeling that she had somehow stepped into a parallel universe where her best friend was ignoring her and her angry ex was now feeling friendly towards her. Not knowing what else to do, she smiled back as Jack waved for her to stay in the car and hopped round to the passenger side before easing himself in.

'Hi, Rachel. Thanks for this, again,' he said, looking down and arranging his crutches in the small footwell.

Rachel stared. What had happened to surly, this-is-all-your-fault Jack?

'No problem,' she answered when he looked up, realising that she should be saying something but not knowing what.

Rachel pulled the car out into the traffic and headed in the direction of the physio's, a route she felt she could drive in her sleep, which was probably a good thing as her life right now was rather distracting.

'Did you manage to get hold of Beth?' Jack asked.

Rachel risked a glance in his direction. It seemed a genuine question with no hidden meaning. So, Rachel concluded, whatever was going on with Beth, she hadn't told Jack.

'No,' Rachel replied. 'It's really unlike her. I'm worried I've upset her.' Rachel frowned at both the thought and the unusual reaction she was getting if she had.

Jack laughed, and it was a familiar

sound that brought back more happy memories.

'Oh, please. If you'd have upset her, you'd know about it. Beth's not backward in coming forward.'

Rachel thought about this for a moment. Jack was right; there had to be some other explanation for the lack of contact.

'I should know. She told me exactly what she thought of me when you and I went our separate ways.'

That was one way of describing it, Rachel thought.

'I didn't know you kept in touch.' Rachel said, feeling bad that she was testing the truth of her best friend's words.

'We didn't,' Jack said ruefully, 'I had one long ranty text that told me exactly what she thought, and then she told me she was deleting my number.'

Rachel felt her grip on the steering wheel relax a little. She was wrong to even doubt Beth; they had been friends since birth, as Beth liked to joke, since their mums had met in the labour ward.

'Then why hasn't she rung me back?' Rachel said before realising that she had said the words out loud.

'She probably thinks she has. You know what's she's like. Her life speed is a hundred miles an hour, and she usually forgets the most obvious thing she needs to do.'

Rachel glanced at Jack to see if he was trying to placate her, but he was looking out of the window and so she took it as an off-the-cuff remark. He was right, of course: Beth's life was hectic even by London standards, and she often forgot to do things which everyone else did automatically, like close and lock the front door.

'Maybe,' Rachel said, still unconvinced.

'We could go round there? After physio, I mean.'

Rachel tightened her grip on the steering wheel. There was definitely something weird going on.

14

'I don't think that would be a good idea,' Rachel said finally in reply. Jack had seemed content to let her think about it — not that she needed to. Beth and Rachel didn't really talk about Jack anymore; certainly not by his given name, anyway. Beth tended to refer to him as 'that man', and that was when she was feeling kind. The last time they had spoken on the subject was the impressive lecture that Beth had given Rachel on getting a grip and moving on with her life. Beth had made her feelings about Jack's behaviour very clear, and Rachel doubted the week or so since that conversation had softened her opinion.

'When she texted me this morning she didn't even call me names, so maybe she has forgiven me.'

Rachel had to blink hard at those

words as completely unbidden she could feel tears start to well up. Was that Jack admitting that maybe he had done something that needed forgiving? Rachel had always known that she had played a part in their break-up, but Jack had never so much as conceded an inch on whether he bore some of the responsibility too.

'Sorry,' Jack said, and even without looking Rachel could tell he was frowning. 'Didn't mean to dredge up the past.'

Rachel sighed. That was really the problem: for her, it didn't feel like the past. Even going out with Chris, there had been many reminders of when she had been Jack's girlfriend. She felt a flash of guilt. If she wasn't ready to move on, then was it fair on Chris? But she liked Chris, she really did. He was the first man since Jack that she had even considered she could have a future with.

'No, it's fine,' Rachel said, going for an airy tone but suspecting that Jack could see through it. 'It's just, I don't think I've ever heard you describe it like that.' She couldn't help herself. She knew the sensible thing would be to move the conversation on to safer ground, but it was like an itch that she had to scratch. Maybe if they talked about it, this time without angry tears and recriminations, maybe she could finally move on.

Moments passed and Rachel wondered if it had been the right thing to do. Jack sat in silence, his face turned away from her, staring out of the window. She couldn't read his mood from the quick flashes of him that she risked, taking her eyes off the road ahead. She pulled up at a red light and turned to look at him properly. He seemed to sense her eyes on him, and he turned to her.

'I didn't feel that way for a long time.'

Rachel nodded, not wanting to interrupt him now that he had finally started talking.

'I was in too much pain, I suppose.'

Rachel swallowed down the familiar sensation of heartache that seemed to swell up inside her. Whatever had happened between them, she couldn't bear to hear how he had been hurting too.

'Selfish, I know,' he said, and flashed a tight grin. 'I know you were too — Beth left me in no doubt of that — but I just felt . . . '

His words trailed off, and Rachel knew that he was unsure whether he should say what was on his mind.

'Felt what?' she prompted, steeling herself for more hurt.

'Abandoned, I guess. I'm not sure if that even sums it up. I wanted you there so badly, and when you wouldn't — I mean, couldn't — come . . . well, it was like my parents all over again.'

Jack's voice wobbled a little, but Rachel didn't need that to tell her the emotion he felt. She felt it too, except hers came with an extra-large serving of guilt. But that was at the heart of it.

Jack still believed she simply *wouldn't* have gone with him, when Rachel knew it was nearer *couldn't*. She had wanted to, had worked so hard to overcome her fear of flying, but even the strength of love she had had for him couldn't have overcome that gut-wrenching terror. To compare that moment to the loss of Jack's parents, who had both died whilst working abroad, only added to Rachel's guilt.

'Then, when I saw you again and you seemed to get on the plane so easily, it was like my heart was crushed again.'

'It wasn't easy . . . ' Rachel started, but it was something she had thought about a lot since the day they had jumped from the heavens. Why had she been able to get on that plane? She'd been fuelled by anger and resentment, but surely that wasn't stronger than what she had felt for Jack. He had been the one, she was sure, but somehow the hurt he had caused and the anger she had felt had overridden all her fear and made her jump. But why?

'I guess I just can't work out why you could do that for Chris, on a first date, and not for me.' Jack shrugged as if it was nothing, but Rachel knew there was a lot more emotion behind the gesture. 'Just ego, I guess, on my part. I can see you like Chris, and he is a great guy . . . ' Jack's voice trailed off. 'So maybe that's why?'

There were words left unspoken, and Rachel felt sure she knew what they were: *Why wasn't I enough?* She couldn't blame Jack. It was a question that she had asked herself many times, and never been able to come up with an answer that wasn't about a failure in her as a person, as a partner. She wondered if she had changed, and that that was why she had jumped out of the plane. Certainly the break-up with Jack had changed her in many ways, and not all of them positive.

In a bit of a fog, she switched the indicator on; they had arrived at the physio's: a route which Rachel had thought she could do in her sleep and now knew that she actually could, since she couldn't remember much of the journey. But deep down Rachel knew it wasn't Chris that had got her to jump out of the plane, it was Jack, and that was definitely something she was going to need to think about.

Rachel sat in the same plastic chair and watched as Jack was put through his paces. He was making some real improvements, and Jen was making noises about him being able to start some light weights soon. Jack certainly seemed focused, and Rachel was sure he wasn't mulling over the conversation they had had in the car, but she couldn't shake the action replay in her mind. She could feel the emotions all start to build up and she knew that the physio's was not the time or place for her to start to unpick how she felt; certainly not when Jack was around.

'Ta-da!' said a voice that was so familiar it made Rachel's heart skip a beat. She shook her head to focus on the here and now. When she looked up,

Jack was stood without crutches and no support from Jen, looking like the cat that got the cream.

'Don't get cocky,' Jen warned, but she was smiling too. 'You're making good progress, but we don't want to undo all that hard work.'

Rachel applauded. It seemed like the right thing to do, and to be honest Jack's mood was a little infectious; but then he had always been able to distract her and make her laugh. It was one of the things she'd loved about him. Keeping her smile in place she clenched her fists, feeling like her emotions were going to overwhelm her on both counts.

'You ready to go?' Jack asked, and Rachel realised she had disappeared into her own mind again.

'Yep,' she said, jumping up from the chair so fast that she knocked it over. The resulting crash seemed to echo around the gym, causing many pairs of eyes to stare in her direction. Blushing, she reached down and righted the chair before heading quickly to the exit, avoiding making eye contact with Jack, who she knew would be staring at her curiously.

★ ★ ★

'If you take a right here, I know a shortcut to Beth's.'

Rachel followed the instructions on automatic pilot, and was only dimly aware that a part of her brain was telling her this was not a good plan. She didn't think having Jack and Beth in the same room would be good on any occasion. Especially now since Rachel was convinced there was something strange going on with Beth, but she couldn't think of an excuse not to; so she followed his directions, and in twenty minutes they were looking for a parking space near to Beth's flat.

'This is fine,' Jack said, pointing to a space that would test even Rachel's excellent parallel parking skills. 'I can walk from here.'

Rachel was only half-listening. There

was a car on the other side of the road that she was sure she recognised. She was positive it was Chris's car, and it seemed that fate was only making her life more difficult since the only reason she could imagine his car to be here, in this street, was if he was visiting Beth. Reuniting Jack and Beth seemed like enough of a challenge, but throwing in a new potential boyfriend? That made Rachel want to run all the way home.

15

Rachel climbed out of the car. She had considered refusing to get out, but knew that it would give a very clear message to Jack that she wasn't ready to be in the company of both her ex-boyfriend and one of his friends, who she was seriously considering as future boyfriend material. That was, if she could work through her jumbled feelings about her ex.

'Stop it!' she told herself firmly. 'You're being ridiculous, and the only person who is going to make this weird and awkward is you!'

Jack, for his part, was standing on the pavement, leaning on his crutches and looking at her with concern. Rachel ducked her head down to hide her blush and made a pretence of checking she had locked the car door. Once again she had the feeling that Jack could read her mind, not a comforting thought.

'It will be fine,' Jack said reassuringly. 'I promise I will behave.' Since Rachel wasn't sure whether he had noticed Chris's car, she wasn't sure whether he was referring to the reunion with Beth or the potentially awkward social situation of former and possible future partners being in the same room. Not knowing what to say, she just smiled, and led the way to the steps that descended to Beth's basement flat.

She lifted a hand to press the doorbell, and the 'Ride of the Valkyries' sounded.

'I see her eclectic tastes haven't changed,' Jack said with a grin.

Rachel shook her head.

'No, same old Beth,' she said, but then remembered why they were here. The problem was that Beth wasn't behaving like herself at all.

Rachel could hear laughter inside, but it wasn't until Chris opened the door that her suspicions were confirmed. His face seemed to freeze in place for a second, and if Rachel had been less concerned about the meeting of past and present she might have simply put it down to surprise; however, in her current state, her inner detector was screaming *Guilty!!!*. But why? Rachel knew that Chris and Beth were friends — it was, after all, Beth who had introduced them — so why would Chris worry about Rachel finding him at Beth's place?

'Mate!' Chris said, breaking through Rachel's distraction. 'What are you doing here?' Chris opened the door wide so that Jack could hop past him. 'Rachel, lovely surprise!' he added, in such a way that Rachel felt he was being entirely genuine and perhaps she was the one losing the plot, imagining all sorts. Chris leaned out the door and pulled her into a hug, before kissing her on the cheek. 'Are you sure it's safe to have Jack and Beth in the same room?' he whispered.

Rachel pulled back from the embrace

and could see a wicked light dance in Chris's eyes. It seemed he had the same thought as her, although he was less concerned.

'It was his idea,' Rachel said with a shrug. She had wanted to say more, to explain that she was worried about Beth, who had been ducking her calls; but then Beth's face appeared over Chris's shoulder.

'Well, this is an unexpected reunion,' Beth said; and she was smiling, but to Rachel there was still something not quite right about her. 'Don't leave Rach on the doorstep, Chris, let her in.'

Chris grinned and moved back into the flat.

'I'll grab some beers,' he yelled from the kitchen, even though both Beth and Rachel had already heard the sound of the fridge opening. Beth went to walk into the small lounge, but Rachel reached out a hand for her arm to stop her.

'Are you sure this is okay?' She asked, studying her friend's face closely,

'I mean I know how you feel about Jack but he seemed to think it was okay to call in. I know you haven't seen him since, well you know but . . . ' Rachel stopped, she knew she was babbling and Beth just seemed amused.

'I can't very well lecture you about letting go of the past, and then not follow my own — might I say, excellent — advice.'

Rachel felt like she had walked into a parallel universe: it wasn't a week ago that Beth had been waxing lyrical about Jack's many faults, and now she seemed happy to have him round for a few beers. Her confusion must have shown on her face as Beth pulled her into a one-armed hug.

'Honest, it's fine,' she said, squeezing Rachel's shoulder. 'Now, come on, before the boys drink all the beer.' And Rachel was pulled by the hand into the lounge.

Jack had eased himself into the only chair, which left the low-slung elderly sofa for the rest of the party. Beth moved the mismatched footstool and helped Jack to put his injured knee on it. Rachel curled up on one end of the sofa and took the offered beer from Chris's hand.

'So, how's physio going, mate?' Chris asked, and all Rachel could do was watch as Jack gave a detailed account. If Chris has been able to leave work to get to Beth's place, then why hadn't he offered to take Jack to physio? Rachel frowned into her beer. Maybe it was her overreacting or being paranoid?

Beth came in with a bowl of crisps.

'Do you two fancy joining us for an Indian takeaway?' Beth said as she dragged the lopsided table in front of the sofa and plonked down the crisps.

'Sounds good to me. I've been housebound too long,' Jack said through a mouthful of crisps, 'I can get a taxi home if you have other plans?' he added to Rachel as an afterthought.

Rachel shrugged. 'No plans. I'm in.' Of course she didn't have any plans! Her potential new boyfriend was hanging out with her best friend, so where else was she going to be? Rachel looked to Beth, who wafted the takeaway menu under her nose with a smile.

For a split second Rachel wondered if this had been part of Beth's plan all along. Perhaps she thought some time with both Jack and Chris in the same room would convince her that Chris was the one and that she was ready to move on, especially since Jack seemed so relaxed to be in their company. He was totally unfazed, so maybe she should follow his lead? In fact, she was starting to feel more relaxed herself, until Beth plonked herself down on the sofa in the tiny gap that Chris had left between himself and Rachel. Rachel made a face at Beth, one which she knew she would understand, as she had made it many times before. Beth, not always good at reading signs, sometimes needed a little help. But Beth wasn't looking at her: in fact, she was just smiling at Chris.

Once Beth had scribbled everyone's order on the back of her hand, she searched her pockets for her mobile and, unable to find it, she looked at Chris, who rolled his eyes and handed over his own. Rachel knew she had never hung out with Beth and Chris at the same time before, but this was definitely strange. Beth had always borrowed Rachel's mobile, even when they had been out with Beth's previous boyfriends before.

As Beth leaned forward to make the call, Rachel tried to catch Chris's eye, but she felt like he too was avoiding her.

'They'll be here in twenty. Do you fancy grabbing the plates and cutlery, hon?' Beth said, directing her request to Rachel, behaving as if nothing unusual was going on.

'Sure,' Rachel said, standing up. An excuse to leave the room, even for a moment, was welcome. She couldn't work out what was going on. Beth was behaving strangely, and now Chris seemed to be joining in. And as for Jack

. . . well, Jack seemed to be acting as if the last year had never happened, let alone the last few weeks.

16

Rachel pulled out the drawer where Beth kept her cutlery, and wasn't surprised that it was empty save for a broken bottle opener and a plastic fork. Her eyes moved to the pile of dirty dishes in the sink. At any other time, Rachel probably would have sighed and dragged her friend into the kitchen to at least help with the washing-up, but this was such a common occurrence that she found it strangely comforting. She filled the bowl up with hot water and dumped in a squirt of washing-up liquid before tackling the precariously stacked pots, pans and plates.

'You wash, I'll dry?' Chris asked, making her jump.

'That would be great, thanks,' Rachel managed to say when her heart had settled back into its rightful place.

'What Beth needs is a dishwasher,'

Chris said, picking up the first soapy glass and drying it with a tea towel.

'What do I need one for, when I have you two?' Beth's voice seemed to suddenly appear in the tiny kitchen, and this time it wasn't just Rachel who jumped.

'We've got this,' Chris said, and to Rachel's mind it was a pointed comment — or was she just imagining what she hoped had been the meaning behind his words? 'Why don't you go and entertain your other guest?'

Rachel didn't need to turn round to know that Beth hadn't moved. She wanted to turn so she could see Beth's face and her reaction, but she knew that she was more likely to give away her own thoughts than detect any of Beth's.

'Or maybe you can find him a job to do? Just remember he's injured.'

Beth made a 'humph' noise, and Rachel heard her novelty slippers shuffle away.

'Nice to know it's not just me who gets lumbered with the washing-up,'

Chris said, and flicked a bubble of soap at Rachel.

Rachel glared at him, but there was no malice in it.

'The story of my life with Beth. She makes a mess and I clean it up.' Rachel frowned as she realised that might be true in a practical sense, but it was definitely the other way round in emotional situations.

'Do you think she's okay — Beth, I mean?' Rachel asked, the words out of her mouth before she could consider whether it was a wise question to ask. She turned to look at Chris and his face crumpled into a frown as he gave her question some thought.

'Well, she's always a bit . . . ' He seemed to struggle to find the words.

'All over the place?' Rachel said, and as their eyes met they both laughed.

'You know, that's exactly it,' Chris said. 'But at least you are never bored around her,' he added, and Rachel nodded in agreement.

They continued to wash and dry up

in silence for a while. The kind of silence that was comfortable, and which nobody felt the need to fill with meaningless words.

'Why?' Chris asked.

Rachel was tempted to ask 'Why what?' but she was stalling. She knew exactly what he meant.

'She hasn't answered my calls since our . . . ' She was going to say 'date', but quickly changed her mind. ' . . . our meal out together.' Rachel focused on scrubbing at a pan that had been used to make porridge, to hide her embarrassment. Why shouldn't she call it a date? It should have been, but somehow having your best friend in tow did kind of change the mood.

'She couldn't find her phone to order the food. She's probably lost it,' Chris said, sounding so reasonable that Rachel again felt like she was the one losing the plot.

'Speaking of . . . ' Chris said, before Rachel could try and steer the conversation elsewhere. ' . . . I was thinking something a bit more traditional for our third date.'

The porridge pan fell out of Rachel's hands, as this was the last thing she was expecting Chris to say. It sent a small tidal wave of soapy water over the edge of the sink, and Rachel could feel it soaking into the front of her jeans.

'More traditional than a meal out?' Rachel asked, groping for something sensible to say.

'Well, no, but I was thinking that perhaps this time we could arrange it so it was just the two of us?' Rachel could see his eyebrows forming a questioning expression, and there was a smile tugging at his lips. She nodded, not trusting herself to reply in a grown-up sensible manner, when all she wanted to do was jump up and down and squeal in delight.

'You know,' Chris said in an overly casual voice, 'without ex-boyfriends and best friends watching our every move.'

Rachel looked up at him and grinned. It felt like Chris had read her mind; but, unlike with Jack, this time she was happy about it. Chris leaned in and whispered in Rachel's ear.

'Sunday. I'll pick you up at eleven.' Rachel giggled and nodded, 'And might I suggest that we keep it from our fellow partygoers?'

The 'Ride of the Valkyries' sounded, and there was the thud of Beth's slippered feet.

'Come on, you two!' she yelled. 'What are you doing out there, making forks by hand?'

This was a typical Beth comment, and Rachel felt like the world had somehow managed to right itself. She had a date booked with Chris, a proper date. One without Beth or Jack. A chance for them to spend some time together, alone, to work out if they wanted more from each other. Rachel couldn't wait. She knew she was grinning when she walked back into the lounge, but Beth and Jack had been distracted by food, so Rachel could happily hug the secret and keep it to herself. This was good, she told herself. Maybe a proper date with Chris would help her make sense of everything? If nothing else, she felt certain that she knew where she stood with Chris, and that was going to make the evening a whole lot easier.

It was late when Jack and Rachel finally made it to her car.

'So, that wasn't too bad, then?' Jack asked as he pulled his seatbelt into place. Rachel smiled; she had had a good time, and after the conversation with Chris, she had definitely been able to relax. Even Beth had seemed more like her normal self, although Rachel had had no opportunity to ask why she had been ignoring her calls.

'No, it was fun,' Rachel said, her mind replaying the conversation with Chris, and she couldn't help but smile.

'Would I steer you wrong?' Jack added, and Rachel had to shake herself from the memory. That was a strange thing to say, particularly with their history, but all Rachel could do was assume that Jack was joking; something he used to do a lot, but she hadn't seen recently.

'Anyway, I was thinking . . . ' Jack started, ignoring the fact that Rachel hadn't answered him. 'I know you're off tomorrow . . . ' Rachel opened her mouth to speak, but Jack held up his hand. 'I know . . . it's your day to catch up on your studies.'

Rachel shrugged, wondering where he was going with this.

'I'm also pretty sure that you still forget to eat when you are deep in study mode.'

Rachel nodded. That part was definitely true.

'Well. I would like to thank you for driving me to and from the physio; and since you won't take any petrol money . . . '

Rachel's cheeks coloured as she remember that particular argument. She had point-blank refused his offer of cash, and Jack had been very vocal. Rachel could only think that he didn't want her help to be taken as anything other than a business relationship, like she was little more than a convenient taxi cab, but there was no way she was going to let him pay her. For one thing, the idea of being paid did little to assuage the sense of guilt she still felt; and for another . . . well, you didn't need to pay friends to help you out. Whilst she could hardly categorise their relationship as friendly, she had hopes that it might end up that way, and thought it would help them both move on and leave the pain they felt behind them.

Rachel realised Jack was still talking and she hadn't heard a word he had said.

'So, what do you think?' he said, and Rachel wrinkled her nose.

'Is that a no?' Jack asked, and instead of a rebuke in his voice he seemed amused. Rachel shook her head; the new Jack seemed to have personality-swapped with the old Jack, and it was confusing, even if it was a relief.

'Or am I to take it that you haven't heard a word I said, being lost in some other place or time?' She risked a quick glance in his direction and could see that he was smiling. Without trying, her sheepish expression conveyed that he was right. Jack laughed, and it was a familiar sound. Before, it might have caused a new wave of pain; but right now it just felt comforting, like a much-treasured memory.

'Are you listening now?' he asked. She nodded, and they both laughed. 'I was suggesting that I drag you from the library at around one o'clock for a picnic . . . a thank-you picnic,' he added hurriedly.

Rachel smiled. 'A thank-you picnic sounds lovely.'

And it did. It was only later in bed that Rachel wondered if it was more than just a thank-you for driving him to physio. He seemed to have changed overnight into the Jack that she remembered, the Jack that she had loved. Had Jack felt the change too?

Had he felt some of the tension between them ease?

As she closed her eyes and willed her mind to switch off the replay of their relationship, another thought struck her. Since Jack had invited her to lunch, she hadn't once thought about her date with Chris on Sunday. She rolled over in bed and groaned, pulling a pillow over her head, trying to block out the confusing mixed emotions. She tried telling herself it was just a thank-you lunch, but one thing she knew for certain: she wasn't over Jack, and that was going to make life complicated.

17

Saturday was usually Rachel's favourite day of the week, and not for the reason it likely would be for most nine-to-fivers. For Rachel, studying for her Master's was what made her feel like her life had a purpose. She loved to be in the library early, with only a few other keen students unless it was the summer and finals loomed. She loved to find her favourite desk waiting for her, tucked away in a corner that was little visited by anyone else but had great views of the small local park. But today she was running late — and it wasn't because of anything mundane, like having overslept, but because she simply couldn't decide what to wear, and that was both troubling and annoying. She felt like she was preparing to get ready for an important date, not a day of studying which would be broken up by lunch with a friend. She forced her mind to use the word *friend*, but that was the problem: it felt like so much more.

'You are winding yourself up for nothing,' she told her reflection. 'For all you know, Jack is more relaxed now because you are dating Chris, and that means he feels less guilty.' She frowned at the thought; it didn't exactly ring true, but she knew right now she couldn't really trust her judgement, since her imagination seemed to be running so wild with possibilities.

'Just put on what you normally wear and be done with it.' She was now wagging a finger at herself, hoping that would help, but it didn't seem to. With a sigh, she returned to her wardrobe, tugged out her long black maxi skirt, and pulled it on. Who was she kidding? She knew what she wanted to wear, so she might as well just do it. It was overdressing for studying, but it was her favourite summer outfit and it made her feel good about herself, so why shouldn't she? Perhaps having lunch with Jack had nothing to do with it. Perhaps she was just feeling better about herself; and if that was the case, then she should wear whatever she felt like.

The library that Rachel loved was at Senate House near the British Museum, and her favourite spot was on the eighteenth floor. The library held books in tall glass cabinets that lined the walls, and every floor was double-height with a mezzanine level. Her favourite spot was there, where small wooden desks with a single chair could be found. Most people preferred to work at the computer stations on the main floor, but Rachel always completed her notes by hand before typing them up at home later. It seemed more appropriate when you were studying the folklore of the ancient Greeks. Her desk was beneath the window and had bookcases on both sides, providing a sort of book tunnel that allowed her to push away the distractions of day-to-day life and focus on her studies.

But not today. Today the library didn't have its usually calming effect, and however hard she tried, she couldn't lose herself in her work. She had felt like this before, and the memory of it rekindled feelings that she had thought were long-suppressed. Jack had been her first love. She had supposed herself to have been in love before, but when she met Jack she knew that she had been wrong. The feelings she had for Jack seemed to permeate every part of her life, and so whatever she had been doing back then, he was never far from her thoughts.

Rachel clenched her fists. 'That was then,' she thought to herself. 'You were young and foolish. That is not now. Now, all you can expect is to be friends with Jack. You've finally moved on — don't dig up the past!' The very thought of that made her smile a little, since that was what her passion involved: digging up the secrets of the men and women who lived many hundreds of years ago.

Rachel tried to imagine what Beth would say, and even searched her bag for her mobile phone. Usually she didn't even bother to bring it with her. Everyone knew that she studied on Saturdays; and anyway, she deeply disapproved when modern technology intruded on this part of her life. With a guilty look over her shoulder, to check no undergrads were present who had previously experienced her wrath for using their phones in the library, she started to tap out a message to Beth.

Even as she was typing, she could imagine Beth rolling her eyes. It wasn't as if they had never had this conversation before. Beth, in fairness, had listened to months of Rachel's tale of woe in relation to Jack, and she knew her friend wouldn't appreciate her bringing it up again, particularly since Beth had gone to the effort of setting up Rachel with Chris.

Chris . . . the thought of him made

her feel guilty. Not that she really had anything to feel guilty about, except perhaps the fact that they were going to have their third date — or their first proper date, as Chris had called it — the very next day. Rachel shook her head; she owed herself, if not Chris, to at least remember that fact.

The unmistakable sound of crutches and trainered feet sounded on the wooden parquet floor, and Rachel was sure it was Jack. She had thought about waiting on the main steps, trying to convince herself it was to save him having to walk through the building and then go up in the lift, but she knew that wasn't the real reason. She had made a deal with herself to treat the picnic as a friend saying thank-you and nothing more. Hanging around outside waiting for Jack like a lovesick teenager would hardly give herself, let alone Jack, the right impression.

'I've come to drag you away as promised,' the familiar voice said, and Rachel did her best to pretend that she had been lost in her work. She swivelled in her chair to face him, and suspected that he had seen through her as she saw a flash of surprise which was then replaced by something else, something almost smug. Had he been able to read her as he always had?

'I just need to grab my bag,' she said, dropping her mobile into it and hoping he hadn't noticed something that was so out of character for her and could only be interpreted as distracted behaviour. She made a show of collecting up the sheets of paper that she had spread out over the small desk in the vain hope of giving the impression she had actually been working, rather than daydreaming.

'Do you want to sit while I put these books back? It might take a few minutes.'

'I'm fine. Doing much better, actually. And besides, Jen says that I need to work on my stamina.'

Rachel caught herself staring at him, taking in the better colour of his face and the way he seemed to stand taller. Jack raised an eyebrow as he took in her close inspection. He moved his hands out to the sides, along with his crutches, so that she could get a better look. Rachel knew him well enough to know that he was enjoying the attention. So she made a performance of looking at her watch.

'I can probably manage forty-five minutes.'

'No problem. I have all the food with me, and I thought we could sit out in the park.'

Jack didn't need to add 'like we used to', as Rachel knew they were both thinking it. Not trusting herself to say anything she just nodded, slung her book-bag across her shoulder, and led the way to the lift. Normally she loved to run down the spiral staircases, but she didn't think it would be right to abandon Jack to the lift alone.

Once they reached the wide reception area, which was full of lockers for coats and bags, Jack made his way over to the reception desk and smiled sweetly at the older woman who was sat behind the computer.

'Hello again!' Jack said cheerfully. 'I've found my friend, so I was wondering if I could have my cool bag back?'

Rachel just stared. The reception staff, used to students asking for an inch and then taking a mile, had a firm-but-fair approach which meant they bent the rules for no one — except tall, handsome men in their late twenties on crutches, it now seemed. Jack was playing up an injured-soldier air to great effect, and charming his way to getting what he wanted, as usual. It had been so long since Rachel had seen the Jack effect in action, she had to purse her lips to keep from giggling, which she had been told reduced the impact of Jack's self-proclaimed super-power.

Once the smiling receptionist had handed over the cool bag and assisted Jack in slinging it over his shoulders

— an action Rachel was absolutely sure he could manage by himself — Jack turned his attention back to her.

'Shall we?' he said, now switching from injured soldier to absolute gentleman. With a small shake of her head, Rachel followed him out of the door and walked slowly beside him as he navigated the steps.

Being in their favourite spot on a beautiful sunny day was like stepping back in time. It felt, to Rachel, as if those painful years had just fallen away and they were back as they were, how they always should be.

'So, how's it going with Chris?'

Or maybe not, Rachel thought.

18

Rachel coughed as her favourite freshly-squeezed orange juice went down the wrong way. Jack reached across and thumped her back with such force that Rachel felt like she was folding in two.

'Sorry,' she said, wiping at her watering eyes with a paper napkin. 'What were you saying?' she asked, hoping that Jack would take it as a sign and move on to something other than Chris.

'I was asking how things were with Chris,' Jack said, not to be put off, and Rachel felt his gaze fall on her as she busied herself taking another bite from her sandwich. Why was he asking? she thought. Why did he want to know? This was not what she had been expecting from this near-perfect recreation of when life had been happy.

'Oh, you know. He seems nice, but

it's early days.' She tried to go for light and airy, to make it clear that there were no possible reasons why that question would bother her, but was pretty sure she had failed miserably. She glanced up, since Jack hadn't said anything, and then it seemed that it was his turn to look away.

'He's a great guy,' Jack said finally, but seemed to be addressing his comment to his own sandwich rather than Rachel. Rachel was feeling more and more baffled. Just when she thought she had worked out what was going on, everything seemed to change like a mini-earthquake. She liked to think she knew Jack well, and so the conclusion she could draw from his interest and then apparent need to stop talking about it was that he still had some feelings for her. Ex-boyfriends didn't ask about such things unless they had a reason, did they?

'Were going out tomorrow,' Rachel said, feeling reckless and like testing the theory. 'Just the two of us, you know.

You were kind of there on our first date, which was a little . . . ' Rachel suddenly wasn't sure she had the words in her to describe it.

'Awkward?' Jack's eyes offered understanding, but Rachel was sure his shoulders were sagging just a little.

'Well, yes, amongst other things,' she said, and looked at him carefully, but even with a pause he seemed unwilling to make eye contact.

'And then Beth turned up on our second date.' This did grab his attention, and he raised his head now, looking her straight in the eye. She was certain she could detect a sparkle of something there.

'It's not funny,' Rachel said, feeling slightly put out that he seemed to think her best friend's gatecrashing was amusing.

'No, of course not,' Jack said, appearing to struggle to form his face into a serious expression. Rachel glared and raised an eyebrow.

'No, really, I agree,' he responded,

holding both hands up as if she needed placating, which Rachel guessed she kind of did. 'It's just — it makes sense of something, that's all.'

Rachel watched as Jack seemed to disappear into a memory.

'Makes sense of what?' Rachel demanded, since Jack showed no indication that he was going to share it with her.

'Oh, nothing,' he replied lightly, returning to being all smiles and cheerfulness. Rachel was starting to feel like she had whiplash with his moods changing so fast. 'So, tell me all about this MA. Did you decide on Greeks or Romans?'

And so, Rachel thought, the picnic turned back into an event where two old friends caught up on what they had missed, and neither Chris nor their past relationship was mentioned.

It had been a good day, Rachel thought as she climbed into bed that evening. She felt sure she had figured out her and Jack; or, at the very least, ensured that she had some space to see where whatever she had with Chris was going. There was only one problem: as much as she tried to think about her date tomorrow, all her mind seemed to want to do was to watch reruns of the highlights of her relationship with Jack. She screwed her eyes up tightly and tried to recall the buzz of excitement she had felt when she had been washing up and Chris had announced he wanted a third date. She could remember the feeling, could even picture her own reaction and the light in Chris's eyes when she had said yes, but she couldn't for the life of her conjure up the actual emotion. It was like all the memories of Jack were swamping her and not letting her think about anything else.

She rolled over in bed and stared at the alarm clock. She had been wrestling with all this for hours; now she was going to be tired, and no doubt cross, in the morning, which did not bode well for her date. Rachel mentally reached for the box in her head where she had shut away all the hurtful memories of Jack, and forced herself to relive them. But after what felt like a lifetime, even that didn't seem to be enough to block him out, as it had in the past.

Jack *was* the past, she told herself firmly; they couldn't go back and change it, so she needed to focus on Chris and her future happiness. Repeating the mantra — *Look to the future* — that Beth had insisted she say out loud every time she started thinking about Jack, she eventually fell into a fitful sleep.

In the morning, when her alarm clock went off, her predictions were right. She was tired; worse, she *looked* tired, with heavy bags under her eyes, and the sort of stretched look that spoke of a lack of sleep not due to having actual fun. Since staring in the mirror wasn't helping, she headed for a shower, knowing that she was also feeling extremely grumpy — at herself and at Jack. What right did he have now to suddenly come back into her life and ruin a relationship that had potential? He had no right, she told herself firmly, as she took the time to choose an outfit that was both flattering and pretty. She slipped her feet in to her gladiator sandals and looked at herself once again in the mirror, trying out a smile. Today was about her and Chris, exploring a possibility, and there was no room for Jack.

She was pulled out of her self-lecture by the tooting of a horn, and ran to the front door. Chris's car was double-parked, and despite the fact it was a Sunday morning, there was already a queue forming of impatient Londoners. She held up a hand to show that she was coming, and pulled open the car door.

'Only people in London could get stressed about a queue on a Sunday morning,' she said, and was greeted by a tight smile. Rachel frowned; it was only a couple of cars, surely nothing to get upset about. Chris said nothing, and Rachel wondered if he had been able to read her conflicting thoughts on her face. They drove in silence for a couple of minutes before it became unbearable.

'Everything okay?' Rachel asked, but not really wanting to know the answer.

'Fine,' Chris said, turning to her, and obviously attempting a relaxed smile but failing miserably. 'Sorry, just a bit distracted by something.'

When he didn't elaborate, Rachel wondered if the whole date was going to consist of awkward silences and her asking questions to elicit some form of response. She turned her head to look out of the window, and wondered if the whole thing had been a giant mistake. Had Chris guessed, and was upset, that she might still have feelings for Jack? Or, worse still, had Jack said something? The thought made her angry, but she couldn't deny the little spark of something that flared at the notion. If he had said something, then maybe he did still care: maybe he was hoping for —

'I can't do this,' Chris said, and Rachel nearly jumped out of her skin. Somehow, she had expected him to remain silent.

'Do you need to be somewhere else? Is it work?' she offered, trying not to jump to any of the other conclusions that her sleep-deprived brain was suggesting.

'No,' Chris said, shaking his head but keeping his eyes firmly fixed on the road in front. 'It's nothing to do with work.'

Again, Chris seemed to have lapsed back into his silent thoughts, and Rachel didn't think she could take it.

'Do you want to take me back home? We can do this another day if you are feeling . . . ' Rachel wasn't sure what word to suggest, so she just let her statement hang in the air.

'No,' Chris said, and pulled the car over into a side street off the road they had been travelling on. 'We need to talk, I think. Why don't we find somewhere for a coffee?' He looked at her hopefully, and Rachel nodded, not knowing what to say and equally unsure what was going on.

'Something's come up, you see. Something I wasn't expecting,' Chris said as he manoeuvred his car into a tight space with ease.

'Oh?' Rachel said, feeling colour rise on her cheeks, sure Chris was about to announce that he had spoken to Jack. She wondered if he was going to tell her they couldn't see each other until she and Jack had sorted everything out. The flare of anger was back. How dare Jack make that decision for her! How dare he even suggest it to Chris? Jack had lost the right to comment on her life that day at the airport and every day since.

She made her hands into fists and allowed her fingernails to dig into her palms. Taking a deep breath, she climbed out of the car and followed Chris to a family-run greasy spoon café, whose windows were steamed up so it was impossible to see how busy it was.

'This will do,' Chris said, making it clear that he didn't really care where they went, but he had something he needed to talk to her about and it couldn't wait. He held open the door for her and she stepped into a room filed with plastic-gingham-clothed tables, tightly packed, and air that was heavy with the smell of fried food. Whilst it didn't look like much from the outside, it was clearly popular with the locals; but there was one table free, squashed into a tiny space next to the glass cabinet that displayed various cake and sandwich options. Rachel slid into the seat up against the wall and a man who was almost as wide as he was tall came over.

'What can I get you?'

There were no menus on the table, and so when Chris suggested a pot of tea and a full English each, Rachel merely shrugged her agreement. This was not at all what she was expecting, and a small, slightly mean part of her wished that she had stayed in bed. She was tired, and not ready to have to tackle the Jack issue from a fresh angle, from Chris's angle.

Now they had sat down, Chris seemed to want to do anything but talk. His gaze travelled around the room as if the collection of people eating breakfast were the most fascinating individuals he had ever laid eyes upon. Rachel, despite wanting to know what was going on — she was a fan of ripping a plaster off in one swift movement rather than peeling it slowly — left him to it. If Jack had spoken to him, this conversation was going to be nine kinds of awkward.

When the breakfasts arrived, Rachel could see why the café was so popular. They were generous portions, of course, but the food also looked cooked to perfection, and the smell made her stomach rumble in appreciation. This seemed to be the cue for Chris to remember just where they were and why. He put down his knife and fork, and Rachel looked up expectantly as he uttered the last words she had expected him to say.

'It's Beth.'

19

Rachel stared, sure she had misheard him, and trying to figure out what Beth could possibly have to do with Chris's current dilemma.

'Is she okay?' she asked, her mind suddenly racing with all the things that could have happened to her friend, and wondering why Beth hadn't told her herself. She felt panic rise as the thought occurred to her that perhaps Beth *couldn't* tell her. Perhaps something was badly, seriously wrong.

A hand reached out for hers and gripped it.

'Beth's fine,' Chris said, giving her fingers a squeeze before removing his hand again, as if he felt he no longer had a right to touch her. Now Rachel was even more confused.

'Is this about her not answering my calls and texts? Have I upset her?'

Chris looked pained at this point and seemed to be struggling to find the right words.

'Can you just tell me?' Rachel pleaded. Beth was her best friend, a permanent feature in her life, and she couldn't bear for something to be wrong with her.

'Beth came round to mine last night.'

Rachel nodded. This was hardly news.

'She said she needed to tell me something. She didn't want to, but she couldn't keep it to herself any longer.'

Rachel's eyes went wide. Had Beth said something to Chris about her? Something bad? She shook the thought away. Beth would never do that.

'She feels terrible, worse than terrible. That's why she has been avoiding you, because she didn't know how to tell you.'

'Beth can tell me anything,' Rachel said firmly, needing to say the words out loud, needing Chris to understand. 'She knows that,' she added, feeling more confused than ever. 'She's my best friend. I would do anything for her.'

Rachel looked up into Chris's face and knew that she was missing something important.

'Please?' she said. 'Just tell me.'

'I don't know how,' he replied, and his face seemed to fracture into misery. 'I told Beth she needed to tell you herself, but she begged me to.'

This time Rachel said nothing. There was nothing really to say, and anything she did would merely delay him ripping off that plaster. She watched as Chris seemed to be fighting an internal battle.

'Beth told me she loved me,' Chris said, and after a heartbeat he looked up at Rachel.

Rachel had no idea what expression was on her face. In that moment, she didn't know what she felt: her mind was completely blank. With a start, she realised Chris was still speaking, and she tried to focus on his words.

'It was completely out of the blue. I

mean, we've been friends for years and I love her to death, but I'm not sure if I love her like that.' This time, it was Chris's turn to blush, as if he had suddenly remembered who he was talking to.

'I'm sorry,' he said, his hand twitching as if he wanted to reach out for hers again but was unsure of how she would respond. 'I didn't mean it like that. I like you, Rachel, I really like you; and I have to admit, I was wondering where this might go ...' His voice trailed off, and they sat and stared at each other.

'Say something,' Chris finally said.

Rachel wanted to ask why Beth hadn't told her, but the truth was that she knew why. It was probably the first time in the history of their friendship when she'd known that she couldn't. Rachel knew that Beth would never intentionally hurt her. Beth had set her up with Chris, after all, because she wanted Rachel to move on from Jack, to find happiness; and now Rachel's happiness was threatening Beth's.

'She's terrified she will lose you over this.'

Rachel shook her head fiercely, even though she could feel the tears starting to build.

'She's my best friend.' As if that answered that fear. 'What I don't understand is why she would set us up, if she felt that way.'

Chris shrugged, and Rachel was sure he had asked Beth that very question.

'You know Beth, she is the kind of instant-revelation person. She said she has always loved me, but as a friend, and then . . . ' Chris stopped speaking and ducked his head, probably embarrassed at talking so openly about this very awkward topic. Rachel nodded. Chris was right; this was totally Beth. If she wasn't being attacked by a range of emotions, she would probably have smiled.

'Well, I know how Beth feels,' Rachel said forcing her voice to be calm and even although she felt anything but. 'How do you feel?'

Rachel couldn't be angry with Beth. She was her best friend, and was what she had done any different than Rachel's own battles with her feelings for Jack? She would be a hypocrite if she even allowed herself to think they were. That wasn't the only problem: Rachel wasn't even sure what answer she wanted from Chris. She liked him, really liked him, and wondered if they could have a happy future together — but she also loved Beth, and would always want her to be happy too. And then there was Jack . . .

Rachel rubbed a hand across her forehead. How had life got so messy and complicated?

'I don't honestly know,' Chris finally said, in response to her earlier question. Rachel nodded: that was probably a fair answer in the circumstances, but it didn't help with the swirling tornado of feelings inside her.

'I really like you, Rachel, and I feel

like I'm a terrible person for even talking to you about this. I know it's unfair.'

Rachel managed a small, tight smile.

'It is what it is, and it's not like you created this situation. It's not like any of us did, really.'

Chris took a sip of tea, and Rachel knew he needed a moment to try and think all this through.

'And Beth?' she finally prompted.

'Has sworn that she will never mention it again. That if you and I decided we wanted to be together, she would be happy for us.'

Now Rachel did think she was going to cry. Beth would do that for her, but Rachel also knew that nothing would ever be the same if she and Chris decided to make a go of it. Everything had changed with that one simple statement: 'I love you'. It always did, of course, but sometimes in ways that had the potential to bring great pain.

'What do you want to do?' Rachel

asked. She suddenly wanted to be at home on her own, to process all of this.

'I honestly don't know. I feel like I've been kicked in the stomach, you know?' Rachel nodded. 'I thought I had things figured out, and it was all good, and then . . .'

'I think we all need some time,' Rachel said, 'to think things through, to work out how we feel.' She stood up and pulled out her purse, but Chris waved it away.

'Let's take a week,' Rachel said, thinking that a lifetime was probably not long enough. 'And then talk.'

She saw the concern on his face. 'Don't worry, I'll talk to Beth,' she assured him. 'I won't let her torture herself for a week.' Rachel squeezed his shoulder, 'I love her too, remember.' And then she walked out of the café; but once she was out on the street, she picked up her pace and ran all the way home to the safety of her bed.

★   ★   ★

Rachel had been putting it off, but she realised that she couldn't any longer. She had to look at her phone, and she knew what she was going to find. Beth had gone from avoiding her to bombarding her with texts and voice-mails. The tone ranged from begging to pleading for forgiveness, and Rachel knew that, however she was feeling, she needed to speak to Beth. To put things right between them. Whatever else was going on, Beth was the most important person in her life, and she wouldn't risk letting her suffer — not when she had it in her power to do something about it.

She picked up her phone and speed-dialled Beth's number. It rang once before it was answered.

'Are you okay? I'm so, so sorry!' Beth's voice wailed. 'I'm a terrible person. I should have just kept my mouth shut!'

'It's okay, Bethie,' Rachel cut across her friend, knowing that if she didn't she would have to wait minutes, possibly hours, for a gap in the monologue.

'But it's not really, is it?' And this time Rachel could hear the tears in her friend's voice.

'Where are you?' Rachel asked, knowing that they needed to be in the same room to have this conversation: neither of them were particularly keen on speaking on the phone at the best of times.

'On your doorstep.' Beth sniffed, and now Rachel laughed — she should have known.

'How long have you been there?' she asked, walking towards her front door and opening it.

'Since Chris texted me to tell me he had told you.' Beth spoke into her phone even though Rachel was standing right behind her. She turned, and her face showed a night-time of no sleep and deep upset. Whatever other feelings Rachel had for her best friend in that moment, love won, and she pulled her to her feet and into her arms.

20

They stood there on the doorstep, arms wrapped tightly around each other, and all Rachel could think of was how much she had missed her friend over the last few weeks. She knew in that moment what she had always known: Beth was her best friend, and she would do anything for her. There was nothing worth losing her.

'Let's go inside,' Rachel said finally. 'I think we both need a cup of tea, and I have some of those biscuits you like.'

Beth's crumpled face seemed to light up at the words. Rachel knew her so well. Her delight wasn't at the fact that she had just been offered her favourite biscuits — it was that Rachel always kept a stash of them in case of an emergency. Somehow, the small things in friendships represented so much more, Rachel thought as she led Beth by the hand into her tiny flat.

With the kettle boiling, the wrapper on the biscuits torn and the first one consumed, Rachel turned to inspect her friend. Beth certainly looked like she had been worrying herself sick, and it was not a state that Rachel liked to see, especially when she felt partly responsible. This wasn't how it was supposed to work. Rachel and Beth had never fought over anything; it had always been the two of them against the world, providing tea and sympathy and a listening ear.

'Why didn't you tell me, Beth?' Rachel asked before realising that she had said the words out loud.

Beth looked guilty, but with a second biscuit halfway to her mouth Rachel wasn't sure whether it was due to that or the fact that Beth had kept something so important from her.

'I couldn't,' Beth managed to say. Her voice was small and seemed to have to fight its way out of her mouth to be heard. Rachel shook her head.

'I thought you knew that you could tell me anything.' She poured the boiling water onto the teabags sat in their favourite mugs, and wondered if that was actually true. How would she have reacted if Beth had told her? She wasn't sure.

'You seemed really happy, you both did. And I was the one to set you up. How terrible of a friend would I be if I then announced that Chris was the love of my life, but I'd only just realised it?'

'Well, you'd be Beth,' Rachel said, smiling a little despite everything. 'As Chris said, you are kind of the instant-revelation person.'

'Chris said that?' Beth asked, and the look of hope on her face was enough to convince Rachel that what her friend felt for Chris was very real. She nodded and smiled, trying to keep the sadness from her face. Somehow, without being told, she had a feeling she knew how this would all turn out. The only question remaining was whether they could all find a way to still be friends when it was settled.

'I meant what I said.' Beth's voice had a fierce edge, the tone that Rachel found so comforting when Beth was leaping to her defence. Rachel looked up: Beth's eyes were bright, and Rachel thought she could make out the tears that were being held back. She didn't have to ask what Beth meant, she knew. They had always been so in tune.

'I know,' Rachel agreed, and they stood there in her little kitchenette and stared at each other.

'I guess we will all know in a week,' Beth said, and Rachel knew that Chris had told her everything.

'I guess we will,' Rachel replied, not knowing what else to say. Not that there *was* much to say, either; ultimately, it seemed it would be down to Chris to work out his feelings. Beth certainly knew hers, though Rachel wasn't so certain; but felt that, given a chance, she would like to explore what Chris and her might be.

'I've missed you,' Beth said, and it

sounded like a question, as if she was testing the waters.

'I've missed you too,' Rachel responded with a smile, relieved that for now at least they could move on to something different.

'Well, you need to tell me everything that has happened to you, and then I will tell you all about me — minus the obvious,' Beth said. This time, her usual cheeky smile was firmly back in place, and she looked much more like her old self.

It was late when Beth finally left. Rachel was worn out, but had a feeling that sleep would be elusive. So much had happened in one short day, and she'd had no time to try and pin down her mixed emotions.

She climbed into bed, piled pillows behind her, and grabbed the notebook that she kept on the wonky bedside cabinet. She wrote down three names: *Chris, Jack* and *Beth*. She stared at the page for a while and scrubbed out Jack's name. Jack had nothing to do with this decision. This was about her and Chris and Beth.

Quickly, before she could chicken out, she wrote a list of all the things that she liked about Chris — and it was a long list. He was funny and caring and seemed interested in her. She leaned her head back against the wall and allowed her imagination to wander. She could picture herself with him, sharing her life and being happy. But did she love him? Did she feel for Chris what she had once felt for Jack?

The thought of his name made her sit up and open her eyes. Jack: it always seemed to come back to Jack somehow, and she couldn't pin down how she felt about that. For the longest time after they had parted, she had yearned for him to walk back in to her life. She would have done almost anything to find herself in the situation that she was in now. Her heartsick mind had known so certainly back then that he could make her happy; but now — now she wasn't sure. Should she risk going back to something that hadn't worked in the past, that had caused her so much pain she'd thought it would end her? Or should she look to the future with Chris, explore what they could be?

Her eyes moved to the other name on the page: the one that hadn't been scribbled out, and the one without a list next to it. Even that decision wasn't simple. She would never be able to consider a future with Chris without thinking about how it might affect Beth, however much she'd reassured Rachel that she would be fine.

Suddenly overwhelmed with tiredness, Rachel wriggled down under the covers. One thing was for sure: she wasn't going to reach any more conclusions tonight, although one glance at her phone told her it was actually tomorrow already.

Rachel's alarm clock sounded like a drill sergeant yelling at some new recruits, and when she reached over to turn it off, it fell to the floor with a crash. The yelling was now somewhat muffled, but not enough to ignore it and go back to sleep. She had no idea how she was going to get through the day, having convinced herself that she had fallen asleep only moments before the drill sergeant started his wake up call. Limping into the shower, hoping it would magically restore her, she heard her phone beep but decided to ignore it.

Standing in the kitchen with her wet hair wrapped in a towel and a steaming cup of coffee cradled in her arms, she reached for the phone. She knew it wouldn't be Chris; they had agreed to take a week to give them both time to figure out what they wanted. It might be Beth, which was a more reassuring thought; it would mean that at least part of her life was back to normal. What she hadn't expected was a text from Jack, quite possibly the last person she wanted to hear from. The very sight of his name, now thankfully without the photograph that she had deleted on Beth's insistence, was enough to send all the whirling emotions of the night before into a frenzy.

Rachel closed her eyes, thinking that ignoring it might be the best option, but then her phone sounded again. She opened one eye slowly, hoping to see Beth's name or even a random text telling her that she had outstanding PPI, but no. It was Jack's name again. With a sigh, knowing that he would not be ignored this morning, she looked at the text.

Hey, just checking you are still on for the physio run later?

And then:

You okay?

Rachel knew without asking that Chris had spoken to Jack. It was bad enough trying to figure this out with just Chris and Beth, but now Jack was involved too. She closed her eyes again, wishing she could go back in time a few days, before Beth had told Chris — or maybe even before she had been on a date with Chris. If that hadn't happened, she doubted she would have ever crossed paths with Jack again. They had, after all, successfully avoided each other for months, despite the fact that they had many friends in common.

There was another beep.

I can tell you're reading my messages, you know . . .

Rachel smiled. She didn't want to. She wanted to be angry with Jack for making a complicated situation even more complicated, but she knew deep down it wasn't really his fault; and, as he always had, he seemed to know what to say to make her feel better.

Sorry. Late night and not much sleep, so a bit slow this morning. Later is fine. Rachel didn't think it had ever taken her so long to compose a simple message, but she wanted to get it right. She wanted to give the impression she was fine so she didn't have to have that conversation. She wasn't ready for it, and part of her wondered if she ever would be.

There was enough of a delay that Rachel was starting to think that maybe

Jack was having the same problem composing a text. Her phone beeped, and a text message appeared, but with no words — this time, there was a link to a video. Rachel clicked on it, and watched a cat fall asleep and roll off a sofa a few times.

Jack had done it once again: knowing Rachel's delight at the silly things in life, he had managed to cut through the noise in her head and make her laugh. She had forgotten what it felt like to have someone so tuned in to her emotions. It was a bittersweet feeling, like a long-lost memory that was precious but was never going to be felt ever again.

One more look at her phone told her that she was going to be late, and so she rushed to dry her hair and tried not to think too much about how she was going to get through the car journey with Jack later.

21

When Rachel arrived outside Jack's flat, she realised that he was waiting for her on the top step, but something was missing. She watched as he carefully navigated the steps down to the pavement, and she knew what it was — he was walking without crutches. Rachel had seen him practice in the gym, but never outside.

'Ta-da!' Jack said, throwing his arms wide when he reached the bottom step. Rachel jumped out of the car.

'Should you be doing that?' And without thinking she reached out a hand to steady him, in case he should start to wobble and risk a fall.

'I'm fine,' Jack said, rolling his eyes. 'I thought you'd be impressed.' Rachel could see the grin tugging at the corners of his mouth, and knew that her reaction had been exactly what he was expecting. So she gave him 'the face'.

'I just wanted to show you that all your ferrying me about has been worth it,' he said in mock hurt, which Rachel could easily see through.

'Yes, yes. Very good,' Rachel said, trying not to smile but failing. 'Get in the car or we'll be late.' She waited for a moment and watched as he got into the car, telling herself she wanted to be sure he was okay, but knowing in reality that she needed a moment. With a deep breath, she climbed in and reminded herself of her plan. She was going to keep him talking, ask lots of questions about the new surfing season and where all the big competitions were. She wasn't going to give him space to ask her anything. She opened her mouth, and then her brain registered that Jack was speaking.

'So, how are you?' The question floated across the space between them as Rachel pulled on her seatbelt.

'Fine,' she said, desperately trying to think of one of her pre-rehearsed questions to ask to throw him off. A hand reached across and briefly squeezed hers, and Rachel had the feeling that her carefully crafted plan was a failure before it had started. She swallowed the sudden lump in her throat and then turned to face him.

'Really,' she said, turning the key in the ignition. 'Really, I'm fine.'

She could feel him study her face, and so she kept her focus on the road ahead and allowed him to inspect her, praying that she wasn't giving away any of her inner turmoil.

'You're a better person than me,' he said, and this was so not what Rachel had expected him to say that she nearly clipped the wing-mirror of a parked car and had to force herself to concentrate.

'What do you mean?'

'Seriously, if my best friend announced that he was in love with the woman I had just started dating, after he had set me up with her . . . I've no idea what I'd do.'

'Well,' Rachel said carefully, 'if they

213

were really your best friend, you would try to understand that they weren't trying to hurt you, but that life is complicated sometimes.'

There was quiet in the car, and Rachel couldn't work out if Jack agreed with her or was stunned into an incredulous silence.

'Like I said, you're a better person than me. I know you love Beth, but seriously? You and Chris are just starting out, and you seem good together, and then — *bam*!' Jack slapped his hands together and the noise was so loud it made Rachel jump in her seat.

'Beth has said she won't mention it again if Chris and I decide to carry on dating.' Rachel winced; she had used the 'if' word, and that was probably a mistake.

'Apparently, Beth is a better person than me, too,' Jack said. Rachel wondered if he was being sarcastic, but when she glanced at him he was looking out of the window, lost in thought. She

214

could feel all her poise drain out of her. Jack hadn't said it, but she knew what he was thinking. He was thinking about what had kept her awake most of the night: would her friendship with Beth survive Rachel continuing to date Chris? She gripped the steering wheel tightly and blinked, trying to hold back the tears that threatened. It seemed so unfair, not just to her, but to Chris and Beth too. Whatever choices were made, it seemed inevitable that someone was going to get hurt.

'Sorry,' Jack said, and his hand reached out for hers, her knuckles white with the tight grip she had on the steering wheel. 'I'm not trying to make this more difficult. Just trying to be a friend . . . but I'm guessing I'm the last person you want to talk to about any of this.'

Rachel drove in silence as she considered this question. And it took only a few moments for her to reach a conclusion. Actually, Jack *was* the person she wanted to talk to. Normally

Beth would be the one, but clearly that was not going to help any of them. Jack knew her, Jack had understood her once, so maybe Jack was the right one for this.

'But I'm here for you if you do want to talk. If you just want someone to listen.' Jack said, once again appearing to read her thoughts.

'Wouldn't it be awkward?' Rachel said, voicing her concerns out loud.

'Not if we agree it won't be,' Jack said, and Rachel had a feeling that he had changed — not just for the worse, as she had first thought when they were reunited, but for the better too. He was not the same person he'd been at that airport, any more than she was.

'We were friends, weren't we? Before we got together?'

Rachel nodded. From the moment she had met Jack, she had known that she wanted them to be more than just friends; but he was right, somehow they had managed to navigate that space between friends and being more quite successfully, for a while at least.

'Why don't we grab something to eat after my physio? Then you can talk about it if you want to, or not if you don't.'

Rachel didn't answer. She was still trying to work out if she could even have that conversation with Jack — after all, it wasn't as simple as he seemed to think. His presence in her life was another added complication, and not one she had been able to figure out.

'Come on, Rachel. You have to eat!'

When she glanced across at him, he was grinning cheekily, and she knew that he had won her over. He had always been able to do that so easily that she wondered if she should feel embarrassed.

'Fine. Food, yes. Talking about Chris and Beth, I'll think about.'

Jack seemed to interpret this as a win, and continued to grin before talking happily about his plans for the start of the season. It was good to hear him be so positive about it, and not just because the guilt that Rachel felt seemed to fade with each moment. It was good because it was like having the old Jack back.

Rachel turned her head to one side as she thought about that. It wasn't the old Jack. He was different, just as she knew she was, but she could still see and hear the Jack that she had loved; and she was grateful that that part of him hadn't been drowned by the pain and upset of their split.

After Jack's physio, they sat in a small Chinese restaurant just around the corner from his house. It had been a favourite haunt of theirs, and that fact was not lost on Rachel. But then, she loved the food there, and the fact that it was reasonably priced for this part of London never hurt either. When they had walked in, they had been greeted like old friends before being shown to their favourite table, Rachel couldn't help but be suspicious that Jack had arranged all this before she had agreed, and she wasn't sure if she should be pleased or a little put out. As it always had before, *pleased* won the argument in her head.

'The usual — or have your tastes in Chinese food changed as much as your desire to jump out of planes?'

Rachel was prepared to glare at him, to give him the look that told him she didn't want to fight with him anymore; but when she looked up his grin was firmly in place, and so she simply raised an eyebrow and smiled before giving her order to the waiter.

'We haven't decided whether the topic of Chris and Beth is on the table, but we didn't say anything about you and me.' His tone was softer now, and Rachel felt panic rise inside her. This was a mistake. She didn't know what she felt about Chris, not to mention Beth, and talking to Jack was like asking two warring mothers-in-law to agree on the place settings at a wedding. She had no idea what Jack felt for her anymore, and part of her was scared to find out.

She had almost decided that she needed to think about her and Chris first, then worry about Jack; but now it seemed she wasn't going to be given that choice.

22

Rachel forced herself to look up, knowing that she couldn't put it off any longer. She didn't know what she expected to see. Maybe Jack was joking? Maybe he was trying to lighten the mood by pretending that he still had feelings for her. The real problem was, Rachel wasn't sure that she knew what she wanted him to say.

'By the look on your face, I'm guessing I've thrown a spanner in the works?'

Rachel reached for her glass of water and took a sip.

'Do you really want to talk about the past?' she asked. 'You've seemed pretty angry about it before.'

She risked a peek at him and knew that she had his full attention. She took a deep breath.

'I've liked having you back in my life,

Jack. I would hate to throw away our new friendship by raking up past hurts.'

Jack paused before answering as the waiter brought dishes of food and arranged them on the table.

'It's been good having you back in my life, too. I've missed you.'

Rachel waited, knowing that he was ignoring the key part of what she had said.

With a sigh, Jack continued: 'And you're right. I was angry. Not that you were dating Chris,' he added quickly. 'I was glad that you had been able to move on, even if I hadn't.'

Rachel stared, thinking about the woman at the skydiving centre with the wild hair. The one who had called him 'Jackie'. It must have been written all over her face, because Jack laughed as if he could read her thoughts.

'Aurora? Really, Rach, I thought you knew me better than that? So not my type.'

Rachel blushed and felt instantly foolish. Not a comfortable feeling, and one that reminded her of the less-happy parts of their previous relationship. A hand reached across the table for hers and gave it a squeeze.

'Sorry, I didn't mean to make you feel . . . ' His voice trailed off as he gestured at her pink cheeks with his free hand. 'It's just that since everything ended . . . ' He squeezed her hand one last time and then returned to eating a spring roll. 'Let's just say, it hasn't got better with time. Some days it felt like that day at the airport had just happened, even months later.'

Rachel nodded; she knew that feeling only too well.

'Chris was my first date since . . . ' she offered

Jack nodded.

'Beth told me.'

Rachel frowned.

'When?'

'She came to visit, after the accident.'

Rachel's eyes were wide. Beth had sworn that she would walk past Jack on the street if she saw him again, so why had she been going to see him?

'Yep, I was surprised too. Especially when she called me all kinds of an idiot, and told me that I should be grateful you were willing to help me out with the physio trips, and to stop being such a . . . well, let's just say she had some choice words to describe me.'

Rachel was confused — not that Beth had leapt to her defence, for that had been her role in their friendship since primary school, but that it all still didn't quite add up.

'She also pointed out that if I felt that strongly about you, I ought to take some time to think about why I was so angry.'

A penny seemed to drop in Rachel's mind, like another piece of the puzzle had fallen into place. It certainly explained his sudden change of attitude towards her.

'And did you?' Rachel asked, her voice so quiet that she wasn't sure Jack would be able to hear her. 'Did you think about how you felt?'

Jack nodded. 'Angry and hurt. Not about the accident, really; more about how you could get in a plane for a person you had just met, but you couldn't do it for me.'

'It wasn't quite like that,' Rachel said dryly. They had already covered this ground.

'I know,' Jack added quickly, and smiled. 'You explained that — '

Rachel cut him off. 'I got in the plane because I was angry with you. I was so angry that it seemed to smother the fear.'

Jack blinked several times and said nothing. Rachel could see he was struggling to process this latest piece of information.

'I'm not sure if that's a good thing or a bad thing,' he said at last, and Rachel had to agree with him.

'I guess Beth's right, and we both need to take some time to think about why we felt so strongly.'

Jack nodded, and picked up his beer before taking a drink.

'Are we angry because of all the unresolved issues, so we just need to talk about them and then move on?' He let the statement hang in the air, and Rachel knew what was coming next. 'Or are we angry because we still care, and perhaps we want to be together again?'

Rachel could feel Jack's eyes studying her, and knew she had to look up: she just wasn't sure what she wanted to see. Hope, she had told herself many times before, was a dangerous thing. It could promise so much, even convince you to believe in happy-ever-afters; but when the person you were hoping for didn't ring or send a message, well, the pain seemed so much worse. But she did look up, and Jack's face told her exactly what he felt.

'I know this is a bit of a bombshell,' he said, before she had a chance to speak. 'And I know that you have a lot to think about.' She could feel him studying her expression, but she had no idea what her face was telling him. 'I know you had a lot to think about before, and I'm sorry if what I've just said makes that more difficult, but I also know I need to tell you.'

Rachel nodded, not trusting her voice to speak for her.

'I'm not asking you to decide now, and I know that maybe you've already made up your mind. Perhaps you've decided that Chris is the one; and if you have . . . well, then I'm pleased for you, pleased for you both.'

Rachel blinked. Jack was talking so fast now, and she had the feeling that she wasn't required to make any comment; that seemed to be the safest approach, judging by the storm of emotions she was currently feeling.

'And if that is the case,' Jack carried on, 'I would really like to be friends with both of you, and I promise I will do my best not to make that difficult.'

Rachel was nodding, trying to keep up with Jack's train of thought, but all her mind could think about was the look on his face when he had told her — or, rather, not told her.

'I also wanted to tell you that I'm off to start pre-training, and I fly out on Monday.' He added this last fact somewhat sheepishly, but it was enough to bring Rachel's attention right back to that moment.

'But, physio . . . ?' was all she could think to say.

'Don't worry.' He smiled. 'I'm sticking to the programme out there, but I'm going to start doing some swimming.'

Rachel opened her mouth to point out that he could easily do that here, but he held up his hand, again as if he could read her thoughts.

'Sea swimming, Rachel. I need to get back out on the board. Following the programme, of course.'

Rachel nodded. She knew enough about surfing to know that the English Channel was not the best place to get back into swimming after an absence like Jack's. But this was all too much. She had so much to think about — too many decisions to make, and no time to make them in. How had life gone from being about getting through the day and wondering what the future would hold to having to make these life-changing decisions, all in a matter of weeks?

'I fly out on Monday. I have to be at the airport by 14.00. I'll have my phone on till I get on the plane. I'm not expecting things to go back to the way they were, but if you would like to see what we could be again, then maybe call me?'

Jack stood up, and it was so unexpected that Rachel jumped. Where was he going?

'I've paid the bill, and it's only a short walk, so I don't need a lift.' He hesitated as if trying to work out the appropriate way to say goodbye to your ex-girlfriend, who was currently dating one of your friends, but you had just declared you still loved. With a soft smile, he leaned in and kissed Rachel's cheek.

Rachel remained where she sat, too

dazed to do anything but watch the man that she had once loved with all her heart walk out of the restaurant. She was still staring long after Jack had disappeared from view. Her mind seemed completely blank now as if she had no thoughts left. She reached for her glass of water, and drank. She had to try and figure out what she wanted, to try and work out what the right decision was amongst the array of options before her, and she didn't have much time to do it. But she knew one thing: she wasn't going to be able to figure it out here. She needed to go somewhere she could think in peace and quiet, with limited distractions. So she headed to the one place that was her home away from home: the library.

23

If you were a postgraduate student, you could access the library twenty-four hours a day, and this was not the first time that Rachel had spent all night there. Usually, of course, it was to study; but this time it had been to think. Rachel used a technique that her mum had taught her, which involved drawing spider diagrams of pros and cons for each decision, which her mum claimed allowed you to see the right answer more clearly. But this time all Rachel had was a mass of lines and scribbled words, and several pieces of paper that she had stuck together with some Blu Tack she had borrowed from one of the poster boards.

The problem was, she thought, as she watched the sun start to appear over the cityscape outside, that all of the decisions were connected. It wasn't like she was trying to make one choice in isolation, and these particular dilemmas weren't like 'Which university shall I chose to do my postgraduate course?' This was 'Who do I love?' And answers to questions like that were never simple. The only conclusion that she had come to so far was that she liked Chris and could see a future with him, and that she had loved Jack but she wasn't sure if they could have a future, after everything they had been through. And casting a shadow over everything was Beth. Their friendship was so important to her that she couldn't ignore the fact that Beth *was* clear about who she loved.

Rachel stared down at the stack of papers haphazardly linked together, and with a sigh she rolled it up before glancing at her watch. It was nearly half-past six, and if she didn't hurry she was going to be late for work, especially if she wanted to nip home for a shower first. She used her pass to let herself out through the main doors, smiling at the security man, who nodded back. In the city that never slept, the streets were busy with people coming from work and those heading that way. Almost everyone seemed to be in motion — except for one person sat on the bottom step, holding a cardboard carrier with two paper cups in it.

Rachel walked slowly down the steps as her memories of the hundreds of other times Jack had been waiting for her after an all-nighter played in her head.

She frowned, remembering the conversation from the night before when he had said he would give her space. He turned his head then, as if he knew that she was standing behind him.

'I know, before you say anything. I said I would give you time to think.'

Rachel nodded and then slowly moved so that she was sat beside him. Jack handed her a cup, which was warm and from her favourite coffee house.

'Breakfast?' he asked, offering her an almond croissant, another favourite post-all-nighter. She took it from him just as her stomach rumbled in appreciation, and he smiled.

'How did you know I'd be here?' she asked, curiosity overriding all the other questions.

Jack shrugged. 'Just a guess. I didn't follow you, or anything,' he added, as if he was worried that he had given that impression. Rachel smiled as his face creased with anxiety.

'Relax,' she said. 'I'm just a little surprised.'

'Good surprise or bad surprise?' he asked, and then brushed a hand across his mouth as if he were regretting the decision to speak the words out loud. Rachel took a sip of coffee as she considered her answer.

'Good,' she said with a smile, as she realised that was the first thing she had been sure about in the last twenty-four hours. Jack's smile was light, and his eyes seemed to sparkle as if fireworks were going off and he had caught their reflection.

'I know you come here to think, and I figured you had lots to think about.' Rachel caught his quick glance at the rolled-up paper she held in her hand. 'Am I allowed to ask what the spider diagrams say?'

Rachel watched as commuters in suits rushed past, phones practically glued to their ears and their minds racing as they started their working day before reaching the office.

'I'm not sure,' she said honestly. She looked at Jack. There was a flash of something. Disappointment, perhaps? Rachel wasn't sure. Maybe she had imagined it.

'So, the library's magic didn't work?' he asked, and she smiled. He had seemed to understand her love of studying and learning, even if he didn't share the passion, and had never complained once about the time she spent at the library.

'Not this time.'

They sat in silence as they watched people and cars pass by. When they had dated, they would go to the park and people-watch, making up stories about who the strangers were and what their lives were about. A couple walked past, holding hands and talking animatedly.

'Childhood sweethearts,' Jack said, out of the blue, and Rachel laughed.

'Her brother's best friend,' she countered.

'They just met on the train, and it was instant attraction.'

Rachel giggled. 'Their parents didn't approve of their relationship, and he was sent far away. He's spent the last two years earning passage on ships to get back here. She waited for him, knowing that he would someday find his way back to her . . . ' Rachel bit her lip. She had got so lost in the game, she couldn't help but feel that she had strayed over an imaginary line they had set out to avoid talking about their past. She looked at Jack, but he was still watching the couple.

'Maybe they'll live happily ever after,' Jack said softly; and now he looked at her, and Rachel felt like no time had passed at all. She felt as if this were a memory from the happiest times of their relationship.

'I think they will,' she said with a small smile. 'They've made it this far.'

'Right, enough people-watching,' Jack said, with obvious reluctance. 'You need to get moving or you will be late for work.'

Rachel nodded, but stayed where she was. Now she was here with Jack sat beside her, she didn't want to move. Not that she wanted to be late for work; it was just comforting, after a long night of soul-searching, to have some company.

'Come on. If the answer didn't come to you in the magic of the library, it's not going to sitting on its steps.' Jack stood, carefully, and then held out his hand; which she took, allowing herself to be hauled to her feet. Rachel found herself pulled into his arms, and they stood there as if time no longer mattered. She knew that she ought to break the spell, but couldn't bring herself to.

So, finally, it was Jack that reluctantly stepped back. He reached up for her face with both hands, and Rachel had the feeling he was trying to memorise this moment, to save it somewhere just in case, and then he leaned in and kissed her softly on the forehead.

'Sorry,' he whispered. 'That's probably breaking the rules.'

She leaned away from him so she could see his face. He seemed both sad and hopeful, and to Rachel it was like looking in a mirror. With an effort, he smiled, and then took first one step and another before finally turning away.

Rachel watched him go, and it was like viewing an old memory replaying in her head. She remembered the last time. The time at the airport, where they had fought, where he had accused her of letting him down, of not caring enough about him. But this time was different, and Rachel watched him walk away slow and steady, knowing that the library had worked its magic after all.

24

On Sunday morning, a week since she had had the conversation with Chris, Rachel was sat in the window of her flat, watching the world go by. The part of London that she lived in was relatively sleepy in comparison to the rest of the city, but there were still plenty of joggers and people who couldn't wait to get hold of the Sunday papers to watch. She had her phone clutched tightly in her hand, as it had been since she woke up earlier than the sun, and she checked it every few minutes. Rachel had been wondering what the etiquette was in these types of scenarios. Was she supposed to text Chris, or was she supposed to wait until he did?

Rachel had thought it would be easier now that she was sure she knew what she wanted, but the butterflies in her stomach told her that even though she had decided, much would depend on what conclusions the others had come to. It seemed so unlikely that they could all get their own versions of happy-ever-after, but all she could do now was to hold on to that hope.

Her phone finally beeped when she was sipping at her fourth cup of tea, and she was just considering whether it was worth jumping in the shower and potentially missing a phone call.

Hi Rachel. Would you be able to meet me at Coffee Central at 11.00?

Rachel allowed herself a moment to take a deep breath. This was worse than waiting to be told you could start the exam when you had been sat at the desk for ten minutes already.

Of course. I'll see you there she texted back, having deleted it several times looking for the right words. She knew deep down that the words didn't matter, but she worried that she might give an impression that didn't represent how she felt.

She had plenty of time, but decided that walking there would do her good, and so she quickly showered and dressed in jeans and a t-shirt, all the while wondering how Beth was this morning. On any other day she would have texted her or rung her to find out, but she knew she couldn't today — not until she and Chris had spoken, at least. The thought of it woke the butterflies again, and so she grabbed her bag and headed out the door. She needed to be doing something, even if that something was walking. Anything rather than sitting around and thinking of what could go wrong — and, worse, who might get hurt.

Coffee Central was busy with the Sunday-morning crowd eating pastries and sipping coffee, most reading the Sunday broadsheets. Rachel scanned through the window and couldn't see any sign of Chris. It was busy, with only a couple of spaces free, and plenty of people who showed no sign of wanting to leave in a hurry, so she headed inside to bag a table.

It was a full ten minutes before Chris arrived, and Rachel was starting to feel like she had been stood up; but finally the door opened with a ring of the bell and Chris hurried in, cheeks flushed either with nerves or from his haste, Rachel wasn't sure. She lifted a hand and waved to him, and he slipped into the seat opposite.

They talked orders first; Chris insisted on paying, so he headed to the counter and put the order in. Rachel smiled as he retook his seat; and Chris attempted a smile back. Rachel's mind went into overdrive wondering what that could possibly mean, but now Chris was here, he seemed reluctant to have the conversation.

'How have you been?' he asked, and then seemed to wince, as if embarrassed at asking such a question under the circumstances.

'Fine, thanks. You?' Rachel asked, feeling it was the only thing she could say to follow up that enquiry. If the conversation was going to go at this speed, she didn't think she would be able to take it.

The waitress arrived then, and placed mugs and muffins in front of them. This act seemed to still the conversation even further; and so, not knowing what else to do, Rachel started to break up the muffin into bite-size pieces, even though in that moment she didn't think she would be able to eat it.

Rachel risked a glance upwards and caught Chris doing the same. She smiled in what she hoped was a reassuring way, although she herself was feeling anything but. If what he had to say was not what she hoped, she wasn't sure what she would do.

'I love Beth,' Chris blurted out, and then appeared to look completely mortified, his eyes wide, and with a look of such fear that Rachel couldn't help but laugh.

'I know you do,' she said softly; and somehow she had known it almost all along — maybe not from their first date, but definitely when they had all been together at Beth's. It seemed so obvious now.

Chris stared, and it seemed like he had lost all ability to speak.

'You do?' he croaked out finally.

'Yes,' Rachel said, laughing again. 'Which is kind of helpful, since Beth is hopelessly in love with you.'

Chris leaned back in his chair and all the tension seemed to leak out of him. It was like a balloon deflating. He was shaking his head.

'I had this whole speech prepared. I even wrote it down and practised it. I didn't know how to tell you, but I knew I had to . . . ' He stopped, seemingly aware that he was rambling. 'I do really like you, Rachel, and I hope — well, I hope we can still find a way to be friends. It's so important to Beth and me.'

Now it was Rachel's turn to take a deep breath. 'It's important to me too. I like you too, Chris.'

'So you're not too upset? Beth is beside herself.'

Rachel reached over and held his hand.

'I knew I liked you, Chris, and for a while I wondered what we might have together . . . but over these last few days, when I realised that you and Beth were meant for each other, I guess I figured that I had been checking that you were a suitable man for my best friend.'

Chris laughed, and the last of the tension faded from him.

'I felt so bad, like I might have misled you. I had always figured that Beth and I would just stay really good friends, but when she dropped her bombshell . . . '

'It changed everything.' Rachel finished his sentence with a grin.

Chris's face became serious.

'Beth told me how difficult it was for you after Jack, and I felt like I had managed to make that worse by betraying you.' He ran a hand through his hair, and some of the tension was back. Rachel reached for the hand and gave it a squeeze.

'I should probably tell you now that Beth's announcement has had a happy consequence,' Rachel said, feeling the fizz of excitement that she had been trying to ignore. Chris's eyes went wide, and then he shook his head.

'What?' Rachel asked, curious about his reaction.

'Beth was right.' He smiled. 'She went to see Jack.' Rachel nodded; she knew that part. 'She said she was sure that he was still in love with you, and she knew that you were still in love with him. She was just worried that you wouldn't be able to figure that out.'

'In that case, it's probably time that you put her out of her misery,' Rachel said, looking out of the window and knowing that she would see her best friend. There was no way that Beth would have been able to stay away from this — whatever the outcome, she would want to be there for Rachel.

Rachel waved; Beth looked guilty and mouthed, 'Sorry'. Rachel shook her head and gestured for her to come inside. Beth looked like she was going to burst, and seemed to be suffering from all sorts of torment.

'It's fine, Beth,' Chris told her. 'It turns out Rachel and I aren't in love.'

Beth practically collapsed into the free seat and then the shaking started, quickly followed by the tears. Rachel threw an arm around her shoulders and whispered, 'It's okay, Bethie. You were right. I love Jack.'

Beth pulled free as if she needed to see her friend's face to know it was true.

'He loves you,' she blurted out, and Chris laughed.

'I know that too.'

'Have you told him?' Beth said, looking from Chris to Rachel and then back again. The whole world would have been able to see the affection pass between the two new lovebirds.

'Not yet.'

'Why not?' Beth screeched, and several coffee drinkers turned to stare at her — not that she ever worried about things like that.

'Because I have a plan, and I was hoping you might be able to help me with it.'

25

'Are you sure you can do this?' Beth asked for the hundredth time from her seat beside Chris in the front of the car. They had held hands the whole way. Rachel wasn't even sure if they realised they were doing it, but since they had declared their love for each other, they had been inseparable.

'Of course she can,' Chris said, smiling at Rachel in his rear-view mirror. 'Rachel jumped out of a plane, remember? After that, she can do anything.'

Rachel was glad to hear the conviction in his voice. As the miles ticked by, she needed the confidence boost. It had all seemed like a perfect plan, but now she wasn't so sure. She wondered if she should have at least sent Jack a text. She wondered if she was getting carried away with the Hollywood moment that she had carefully crafted; and whether, unlike the movies, it would all go horribly wrong.

'We've got plenty of time,' Chris said as Rachel moved so she could see the dashboard clock, something she had compulsively been doing from the moment she climbed into the back seat.

It was busy, and they had to queue to get into short-stay parking. Rachel was finding it hard to sit still. As soon as Chris had pulled into a space, Rachel was out of the door, pulling her bag behind her. Beth and Chris seemed to be moving at a snail's pace, and Rachel felt like a child at the zoo who wanted to hurry up and go to see the next animal. An arm slipped into hers, and she looked down to see Beth smiling up at her.

'Come on then, Juliet, your Romeo is waiting.'

They joined the stream of people walking towards Departures, pulling suitcases and carrying small children. Rachel steered them away from the moving walkway; it was too slow, and there was no way she had the patience for it. The Departures area was teeming, and Rachel felt a sudden swell of panic. What if they couldn't find him before he went through to board his flight?

'The Quantas check-in desk is this way,' Chris's voice said calmly. They moved down the back of the hall, past queues of people, and found it. The line here was long too, but one glance at the screens told Rachel they were boarding for several flights. Beth slid her arm from Rachel's.

'He's there,' she said, nodding her head in the direction of the queue. Rachel knew it was Jack in an instant, despite that fact that she could only see his head and shoulders above the crowd. She took one step, and then stopped. Memories of the last time threatened to drown her.

'It's different this time,' Beth whispered. 'You're both different.'

Rachel looked at her friend and the

conviction in her eyes gave her the strength to step forward, putting one foot in front of the other. The people in the queue seemed to be moving faster, and it was then Rachel realised that she was running. Running and calling his name.

'Jack!' On the third shout she saw his head turn. He looked confused, and then his whole face seemed to light up. He let go of his rucksack, dumping it unceremoniously on the floor, and spread his arms wide. Just in time for Rachel to launch herself into them. Jack moved into the space between queues and spun her around before gently putting her feet back on the ground, although his tight grip didn't let go.

'You chose me?' he asked, and his voice seemed loud, now that the queue had gone quiet and were enjoying the spectacle they were putting on.

'It was always you,' Rachel said, and could feel the tears coming. But this time they were tears of sheer joy as Jack gently pulled her back to him so that they could kiss. They broke apart when the round of applause got so loud that even they couldn't ignore it any more. Rachel felt her cheeks colour, but Jack seemed only to be proud and unbothered. They stood with their arms around each other as Beth and Chris walked towards them. They embraced as a four, and then shared individual hugs as Rachel marvelled that maybe, just maybe, they could all get their happy-every-after.

'Hey, mate. Do you want to check in or what?' an Australian voice sounded. The queue had continued to move despite the show, and Jack's face fell.

'I can't believe I just find you again, and have to fly out for the season. I'm not going to see you for five months.' He looked desperate, and Rachel couldn't resist a small smile.

'But that doesn't matter,' he said hurriedly, as if he too was worried that they would replay that day from all that time ago. That day when Rachel had been paralysed by terror and unable to get on the plane, despite all the hours of support and effort that Jack had given her to overcome her fear. His face then had shown the most terrible betrayal, but now he just looked bereft.

Rachel reached around him for the suitcase on wheels that Chris had kept carefully hidden.

'It does matter,' she said firmly. 'And this time I'm coming with you.' When she said the words out loud, she knew that she meant them. She knew, for certain this time, that she would get on that plane. She loved Jack, and she wanted to be with him. If she had survived jumping out of a plane, then she could survive another trip, if she had Jack by her side.

Jack looked stunned, and she wondered if she would be able to push him over, as his whole body seemed to have gone slack.

'You don't have to,' he said, pulling her to him. 'I should never have tried to make you last time. I was hurt, yes — but I loved you more than that, and I should have told you.'

Rachel smiled. The past finally seemed like the past now, and this was a fresh start.

'I know I don't; but I want to, really.'

Jack nodded slowly, as if he were afraid to break the spell.

'But what about work and your Master's? You can't just walk away from that.' And Rachel knew that they had both changed. She knew that they weren't the same people they had been. They had grown up, and perhaps now they were ready to love each other completely, including their faults.

'You're right, I can't — but I've negotiated three weeks off work and contacted Queensland University, and they have agreed to let me use their library for my research. I actually think it will add an interesting dimension, looking at local folklore.'

She started to smile at the thought, but then found herself thoroughly kissed once again.

'But the money?' he whispered.

'I never spent it. I kept it. I guess I thought I might need it one day.'

Jack grinned and kissed her again.

'Better get back in the queue, mate, unless you both want to miss your flight!'

Hands were shaken and hugs exchanged, as were the smiles of people who had each found their happiness.

'We'll be here to pick you up,' Beth promised as she gave Rachel one last squeeze.

'Thank you,' Rachel said softly back.

'For what?' Beth asked.

'For knowing me better than I know myself.'

Beth smiled and, letting go of her friend, found herself pulled into Chris's arms. Jack's hand reached for Rachel's, and Rachel knew that the part of her that had been missing had been found. They handed their tickets over to the agent.

'I don't suppose we can get seats together?' Jack said, and there was a fleeting look of worry on his face.

'It doesn't matter if we can't,' Rachel said, knowing she meant it. 'I'll be fine.'

'Don't worry, I saved you two seats together,' the smartly dressed agent said with a smile. 'Good luck!'

'Thanks,' Rachel said. 'But we won't need it!' And she walked hand in hand with Jack onto the plane, knowing that they had both found their happy-ever-after.